Readers Love ᴀɴᴅʀᴇᴡ Gʀᴇʏ

Fire and Water

"In the end, this was a nice romantic little read with an edge of thriller thrown into the mix and I loved the ending. Very sweet."

—Bookpushers Reviews

Through the Flames

"The story build up is done well. The plot moves nicely with danger ramping up until the final moment. And a couple hot bedroom scenes."

—Sparkling Book Reviews

Fire and Sand

"This story is easy and sweet and relatively low angst. If you're looking for a lovely way to kill a cold, winter afternoon, this story will warm you up."

—Love Bytes Reviews

Heartward

"I really felt the author did a brilliant job of balancing the small-town feel with realistic characters, a strong cast of secondary support characters and a lovely, slow-blooming relationship between Tyler and Alan."

—Long and Short Reviews

Fire and Flint

"I love that this series fills me with warmth and strong love. The MC's in this book feel indestructible to me."

—Diverse Reader

Rekindled Flame

"If you're looking for a slow paced, emotional read with a sprinkle of mystery and a happily ever after romance, then I would highly recommend this book."

—OptimuMM Book Reviews

By ANDREW GREY

Published by DREAMSPINNER PRESS
www.dreamspinnerpress.com

By Andrew Grey (cont'd)

Published by DREAMSPINNER PRESS
www.dreamspinnerpress.com

Published by DREAMSPINNER PRESS
www.dreamspinnerpress.com

UP IN FLAMES
ANDREW GREY

Published by
DREAMSPINNER PRESS

8219 Woodville Hwy #1245
Woodville, FL 32362 USA
www.dreamspinnerpress.com

Up in Flames
© 2025 Andrew Grey

Cover Art
© 2025 L.C. Chase
http://www.lcchase.com

Mass Market Paperback ISBN: 978-1-64405-854-1
Trade Paperback ISBN: 978-1-64405-027-9
Digital ISBN: 978-1-64405-026-2
Trade Paperback published March 2025
v. 1.0

To Dominic, for all his support, and to Karen, who is always there with encouragement and a story idea or two.

CHAPTER 1

TO SAY that Chase van Casten was nervous was the understatement of the century. Okay, maybe *nervous excitement* was a better description. He felt as though he was going to jump out of his skin at any moment, even though all he was doing was wiping down the fire engine for what seemed like the eighth time. Waiting around sucked. Everyone was all coiled energy, just waiting to be called into action.

"You need to stop looking like you'll bolt out of here any second," Hayden said as he inspected Chase's work. "Why do you think we take such good care of our equipment?"

"So it's ready when we need it," Chase answered, feeling like he was regurgitating from a textbook.

"That's part of it. But keeping our equipment in working order doesn't mean we need to wash and polish it every day. Hell, sometimes it's a wonder the truck isn't totally waterlogged. Its real purpose is to keep us busy and give us something to do that isn't sitting around looking at the clock, waiting for the next call. It will come. They always do."

"Yeah. I went on one yesterday out to the highway because there was an accident. But all I did was sit around waiting in case something happened." He had hoped there would be some action, something he needed to do, but in the end they'd returned to the station once it became clear the cars weren't going to burst into flames. "It was kind of boring," he whispered.

Hayden looked upward for a second and then laughed. "Being a firefighter is long hours with nothing to do followed by a few minutes of heart-pounding excitement where we need to be calm and collected." He patted Chase on the shoulder, standing tall before stretching, his shirt riding up.

Chase turned away and tried not to react to the strip of warm flesh. Scuttlebutt traveled pretty quickly through the station, and Chase already knew that the other gay firefighter at the station was well and truly taken. Not that he was interested in any sort of relationship. His last one had ended about as badly as possible, and Chase had determined that mindless sex with no commitment or emotional entanglement was the way to go. After all, he was young, strong, and he liked to think good-looking. He was starting to make friends in town, and there were places he could go to meet guys for a good time. That was all he needed.

"Where did you go?" Hayden asked.

Chase pulled his attention back to what he was doing. "Nowhere. Just thinking about shit."

"That can be dangerous, you know." Hayden's tone was teasing.

Chase finished what he was doing and was putting away the cleaning supplies when the alarm went off. Instantly the quiet was shattered, not just by sound, but activity. Chase jumped into his fire suit and joined the others on the engine before it pulled out of the garage and raced through the streets.

This was what a bat out of hell felt like. The truck rocked with each turn, and the air swirled around the open section of the cab as he watched where they'd been. "Two-alarm house fire," Hayden said. "This is not going to be pretty. You know your job, so do it right away."

Chase nodded. He had to get the hoses out and hooked up. They had practiced the routine many times. As soon as the truck stopped in front of the house with black smoke pouring out of every front window and the roof, his feet hit the ground. He sprang into action, pulling out hoses and hooking them into a line. Then Hayden attached it to the hydrant, and Chase began spraying water through the upper windows, sending up a cloud of steam.

"It's burning really hot," Chase said to himself. They had communication through their helmets. Guys scurried behind him, the captain gathering information while Chase concentrated on his job. He moved the stream of water to the second window, sending up more steam.

One of the guys bumped his shoulder, and Chase let him take over the hose, wondering if he had done something wrong.

"Take that hose around to the back of the house," the captain told him.

Without hesitating, Chase dragged the hose through the side yard and around the back. That part of the house was quiet. The fire seemed confined to the front for now. Still, he wetted down the walls and got water up and over the roof.

Looking upward, watching where his water was going, he nearly missed it: movement in the upper floor window. "I need some help back here, now," Chase said, relieved when Hayden raced back. Without thinking, Chase handed him the hose. "There's someone up there."

Chase ran around to the side, grabbed a ladder, and hurried back. He extended it far enough to reach the window before climbing with practiced ease. By the time he reached the window, he had his tool in hand and broke the glass. Smoke poured out of the opening as he cleared away the shards, then entered a back children's bedroom with a small bed, stuffed toys, and a dresser with open drawers. He looked around for a second before slamming the door closed to block out the flow of smoke.

A squeak caught his attention. Then he bent down and looked under the bed into a pair of huge blue eyes filled with panic.

"It's okay. I'm a firefighter, and I'm going to help you." He extended his hand, and the child took it. Chase gently tugged him out and lifted him into his arms. "It's going to be okay," he said as a crash sounded in the rest of the house. Either the floor or roof must have fallen in. Chase didn't have the time to think about it. "Put your arms around my neck and hold tight, okay?" With one hand he held to the boy, and using the other, he got them out onto the ladder. The young boy clung to him tightly, and Chase slowly stepped toward the ground, where a group of the guys waited.

As soon as his feet touched the ground, he hugged the boy, who shook like a leaf against him.

A man raced up to them. "Oh God." He took the boy, holding him and rocking him against his chest.

Chase guided them away from the building and took off his helmet, glad to breathe fresh air.

"Peter, are you okay?" the man said through sobs as he continued holding the boy. He must have been five or a little older.

"Take him out front and let the paramedics look him over," Chase said.

The man looked up at him with huge, piercing blue eyes. "Thank you for saving him." The words were barely understandable. "I left him with the sitter, and when the fire broke out, she got out, but Peter...." He tried to take a step, but his knees buckled.

Chase caught them both. "Come with me. Let's get him looked at." Chase held the man's arm and took him through the large side yard. They picked their way over hoses and around the firefighters to a waiting ambulance.

"Way to go, kid," one of the older guys called when they saw him. Chase kept his mind on the task at hand, getting the father and son to the ambulance, where they sat Peter down and the EMTs got to work.

"Thank you," the man said again, and Chase nodded before reporting to the captain.

"Damn, kid, that was some initiation," the captain said.

Chase nodded. "Why didn't we know about the child?" They could have gotten to him earlier if they had.

"The sitter was overcome, and they had already transported her to the hospital. The father just showed up and told us that his son was inside and then ran around to the back as you were climbing the ladder. What I want to know is how you knew."

"I saw movement inside," Chase said. "I knew it could have been a phantom, a trick of light and smoke, but I couldn't take the chance."

The captain nodded, and Chase stepped away and let him get back to directing the others.

The voracity of the fire was abating. One of the firefighters stood in the open front doorway, spraying water inside.

Hayden came up next to Chase. "You did amazing. I swear you were inside less than two minutes and you got the kid. Well done. I guess you get to come back to work tomorrow." He grinned evilly.

"Asshole," Chase retorted.

Hayden clapped him on the shoulder. "Did you get checked out?"

Chase shrugged. "I didn't get any smoke. I'm good." Hell, he was on cloud nine. His first real fire call and he'd rescued someone. That was why he had become a firefighter in the first place. Chase didn't have a hero complex, or at least he didn't see himself as a hero, but he saw the profession as one that had heroes, and maybe today he had shown that he might have what it took to join their ranks.

The team continued putting water on the building until, after about half an hour, they pulled some of the hoses back and teams of firefighters went inside. When they returned outside, they declared the fire extinguished. Chase joined the rest of the team as they gathered up the hoses, rolled them, and put the equipment away.

Peter and his dad sat on the back of the ambulance, Peter holding his dad's arm while the parent talked on the phone. "I know…," he was saying as Chase drew closer. "Yes, it seems like the building is a total loss. There's only the outside shell standing at the moment, and it's not likely to be structurally sound. Okay. … Okay. … We'll do that. Thank you." He hung up, his eyes a little wild.

"How are you both doing?" Chase asked, kneeling in front of Peter. "Are you breathing okay?"

"Yes. The ambulance man said I'm okay." He leaned closer to his dad before burying his head against his side.

"That's good. And you were brave, staying in your room like that where we could get you out." Chase smiled a little, but Peter didn't say anything more.

"Peter is okay. They said he breathed in some smoke and that I should keep an eye on him for a few days, but he seems to be doing okay and isn't coughing a lot." The man's hand shook a little.

"How are you doing?" Chase asked. "Are you able to find a place to stay?" There was no way this small family was going to be going back into the house anytime soon… or likely ever. Only the back section of the home was still roofed.

"I guess we'll put up at the hotel downtown. That's what the insurance company said to do, anyway." He seemed unsure of himself. "But I want to thank you for what you did. If you hadn't seen Peter…." His voice cracked. "I can get a new house, but…." He shook, and Peter held him tighter.

"It's okay, Daddy. The fireman saved me."

The man lifted Peter into his lap and held him tightly. "I know. You're all that matters." He seemed like he was trying to keep it together. He buried his face against his son, and Chase turned away and left them alone so he didn't intrude.

"How are they doing?" Hayden asked when Chase returned to help with the cleanup.

Chase realized he didn't have an answer. "As well as could be expected, I guess." He couldn't help turning to look at the two of them. "Is it always like this? I mean, there's the excitement and all, but they never tell you about the aftermath."

"You're getting a trial by fire this time, that's for sure," Hayden said. "You good to ride back with the crew?"

"What are you doing?"

"I need to narrow down the cause of the fire. You can help if you like." Everyone said that Hayden was really good that way, and he liked to work with the new team members. "Finish putting the gear away, and we'll take a look inside."

Chase got to work on that, and the captain told him to stay with Hayden and help him out, so while most everyone else packed up and left, including Peter and his dad, Chase pulled on his gear and followed Hayden inside through the back door.

"We're looking for the places where it's burned the most. That will lead us to where the fire started."

Slowly they made their way forward. The floors were charred, and Chase stayed back and let Hayden pick his way through first. It was best to keep their weight spread out.

"Look there," Chase said, pointing to a hole in the floor of the living room. "That didn't just cave in—it was burned away from below."

"Good eye," Hayden praised. "Back up and we'll go down the back stairs. I think we'll probably find what we need down there."

They retraced their steps, water dripping from above as they found the stairs leading down. Chase turned on his light and followed Hayden. Thankfully the stairwell was in the unburned section of the house.

Hayden shone a light through the old basement, their boots sloshing through an inch of water.

"The power has been turned off, I hope." Chase looked around nervously.

"We wouldn't be down here otherwise." Hayden shone his light at the electrical box on the wall. It looked like it had been through a war. "Looks like we found our culprit. Something in the box must have really shorted out for it to look like this."

Chase looked the box over, then wandered to the hole in the floor above before returning to where Hayden was trying to get a closer look at the melted insides. What Hayden was saying made sense, and the electrical box was definitely a melted mess, but he kept returning to the hole in the floor and the debris beneath it. Chase kicked through it a little to see what was under there and located a few melted bits of plastic. The pile was soggy, and it was hard to distinguish what most things had once been. "Check this out," Chase said, kneeling to get a closer look.

Hayden came over. "All that probably dropped through the hole in the floor. You can see it's open all the way through the roof. It's likely this was the weakest spot, and as soon as the fire broke through, it worked its way up, making its own chimney." He returned to what was left of the electrical box to take some pictures and a few samples.

"Did you ever have electrical training?" Chase asked.

"Not really, which is why I'm taking pictures so I can look into it further. But I'm pretty sure this is where it started." He took the photos, and then the two of them left the basement and the house. Hayden made a phone call requesting that the police cordon off the house in case they needed to look into anything more. Then they rode back to the station, and Chase went inside and took off his gear before joining the rest of the team in cleaning off the trucks and restowing the supplies.

AT THE end of his shift, Chase left the station and walked through town to his apartment above Miss Ruthie's Timebomb, a vintage clothing store in downtown Carlisle. He entered the door at the side of the storefront, then climbed the stairs to the second floor, where he showered and decided he didn't want to cook. His mom was great in the kitchen, but that talent had skipped right over him. He could heat things up, but that was about the extent of his skill in that particular area.

Once he no longer smelled of smoke, Chase dressed and wandered down Hanover Street toward one of the restaurants. He was hungry, and the Whiskey Rebellion, part of the hotel downtown, had some of the world's best onion rings. Chase had no idea how they made them, but the batter came out light and crispy. They also had an amazing shepherd's pie, and he loved the stuff. It was almost as good as his mother's, though he would never tell her that. He'd first had those incredible onion rings when he came to town to interview for the job, and now that he'd started, he wanted to treat himself. After all, he'd done well.

The restaurant was busy. Chase checked in the bar to see if there was an empty stool, but everything was taken. He was about to leave when the man from the house fire hurried up to him. "You can join us for dinner if you want." He turned back to where little Peter sat at the table.

"I don't want to interrupt your dinner." Chase could go down to the diner or eat at one of the brew pubs.

"Are you kidding? If it weren't for you, there wouldn't be a dinner at all." He motioned, and Chase followed him to the table.

"I'm Chase."

"You already know Peter. And I'm Jerrod Whipkey." They shook hands, and Chase took an empty chair. "Have they found out what started the fire?" he asked softly.

"We're still working on it." Chase didn't think it was appropriate for him to discuss what he and Hayden had found. "These things can take some time."

"I suppose." Jerrod sighed. "I wish I had been home." He smiled at Peter, who drank from his glass of milk. Chase had nothing to add to that. "The sitter had gotten herself out of the house and left Peter alone upstairs."

"Are you the fireman who rescued me?" Peter asked.

"Yup. I guess I look a lot different now," Chase said as Peter slipped out of his chair and came up to Chase to give him a hug.

"You were brave."

"So were you," Chase said. "You were really brave too." He returned the hug, and then Peter went back to his seat, smiling at his daddy. Chase felt like a hero for about two seconds, but more because of his profession. Any of his coworkers would have done the same thing if they had been in his position. He decided to change the subject. "What do you do for work?" he asked Jerrod.

"I'm an independent electrician. I work on a number of the developments going up around town."

At first Chase was excited because maybe Jerrod could help with the cause of the fire, but then realization kicked in, and he knew that if Hayden was right and the cause was an electrical issue, then one way or another, Jerrod was going to be in a world of hurt.

CHAPTER 2

JERROD SAW the flash of worry cross Chase's chiseled features, but Peter squirmed out of his chair. "I have to go," he said, doing that little-boy pee-pee dance.

"Okay. I'll take you."

Peter shook his head. "I know where it is. I'm not a baby, you know." He hurried out of the hotel restaurant and turned the corner before Jerrod could stop him.

"Excuse me just a minute." He hurried after Peter, approaching the bathroom just as the door closed. He went inside. "Peter?" No answer. He checked the stall and found it empty. An older man stood at the sink, the only other person there. Instantly he turned and left, checking the hall outside, wondering where Peter had gone. His chest constricted with those first seconds of panic that he tamped down because he needed to be able to think.

"Is everything okay?" Chase asked when Jerrod peeked into the dining room to see if Peter had returned. He joined Jerrod in the hall.

"I can't find Peter. He was out of my sight for two seconds." He breathed deeply, trying to think.

"Go ask at the hostess stand. Make sure he didn't go outside," Chase said. "Then check at the hotel desk." Chase went in the other direction.

The seating hostess said that Peter hadn't passed her but that she would watch for him just in case. Jerrod hurried back to the desk, excusing himself as he interrupted the desk clerk with his request.

"A little boy, about this tall with blond hair? He passed us as we came to the desk," the lady in the stylish suit said. "He seemed like he was on a mission."

Yeah, one to give him prematurely gray hair. "Thank you. I'm sorry for interrupting." He hurried away, wondering where Peter could be.

As Jerrod reached the top of the stairs from the lower level, Chase called out, "Jerrod!" He was holding Peter's hand.

Jerrod's panic turned to relief. "Where did you go?"

"To the potty," Peter answered. "Those are yucky," he declared, pointing at the closed men's room door, "and the ones down there smell nicer." He said it as though it was completely logical. "Can we eat now? I'm hungry."

He walked back toward the dining room, and Jerrod looked upward, shaking his head. Something told him he was going to need all the strength he could get.

"He was washing his hands when I found him," Chase said.

Jerrod nodded. "It figures. I'm just wound up." With the fire earlier that had nearly cost him Peter, he was on edge. They had lost their home and most of their things, such as they were, but coming so close to losing Peter had left him feeling brittle.

"You have every reason to be." Chase motioned toward the dining room. "I think you better get in there before Peter decides to order everything on the menu." Chase smiled, and Jerrod nodded his agreement and headed back to the table, where Peter held his menu like he was reading it.

"Daddy, what's gooey meat?" Peter asked seriously, then set down his menu and pointed to the item.

"That's Wagyu beef, and it's really fancy steak. How about we get you some chicken or macaroni and cheese?" He wasn't sure how quickly the insurance company would come through with cash to pay for hotels and stuff, so he needed to make sure the money he had lasted, and that didn't include fifty-dollar steaks for a six-year-old.

"Okay," Peter said. "Chicken and onion rings?" He raised his face with those huge blue eyes shining.

"We can all share," Jerrod said, and when the server returned, they placed their orders. Jerrod got the shepherd's pie, the same as Chase, and soon they were all munching on rice-tempura-battered onion rings that tasted like heaven.

"What's it like being a fireman?" Peter asked. "Do you get to ride on the big truck? Do you have a dog with spots? Do you sleep at the station? Is there a fire pole to slide down?" His eyes were huge.

Chase smiled. "Yes, I get to ride on the big truck, and there is a siren and lights. We don't have a dog at the station. We used to, but not anymore. Sometimes I sleep at the station, but not all the time. And there is a fire pole, but most of the station is on one floor, so we don't get to use it very often."

"Have you been a firefighter for long?" Chase looked young, but Jerrod didn't want to assume anything.

"Today is my second day with the team here. I trained and worked as a volunteer for two years before that, so I have some experience, but to the people here, I'm the new guy, and I probably will be for a while. The people I work with are good. I was a little worried when I first joined."

Jerrod nodded as a familiar flutter rose in his belly. "By and large, the people here are pretty supportive," he said as Chase met his gaze. "I always worry when I bid on a job, but so far most people don't care about my personal life as long as I get the job done right and on time." He hoped he understood what Chase was saying. "I did have a couple issues with a few of the journeyman electricians I hired a few months ago. They found out that I was gay…" He decided to go for the truth and see if he was on the right track. Judging by the smile and the nod, he was. Not that he was in the closet, but he didn't like to make assumptions about others. "… and decided they were going to try to sabotage the job I hired them for." He shook his head. He didn't really want to go over that particular mess.

"One of the firefighters I work with is gay, and he doesn't take any crap, so he's paved the way for me and anyone who comes after me. But there are a few guys who keep their distance and don't talk to either of us very much. It's okay—the captain isn't going to let anyone get away with anything."

"You're lucky to have support." The server brought their entrees, and Peter tucked right into his chicken. There were times when he was a finicky eater.

"I really am. I suppose you're pretty much on your own."

He very much was. There was no one to back him up, and the men he'd hired had gone out of their way to try to cause trouble after Jerrod had let them go, but it had backfired. Contractors talked to one another, and they didn't want to hire troublemakers. "I feel like I am sometimes."

"How long had you lived in the house?" Chase asked after swallowing and setting down his fork.

"I bought it two years ago after Peter came to live with me. That was a really turbulent time, and I needed a home where Peter could have his own room. Peter is my brother and ex-sister-in-law's son. When they divorced, Johnny got custody of Peter. His mother, Gizelle, was in no shape to care for him. She still isn't." He cleared his throat, reminding himself not to go too far down that road because he didn't want to speak badly about Peter's mother in front of him.

"I see." Chase glanced at Peter, who happily munched on one of the onion rings.

"I get a big bed upstairs," Peter said, kind of out of nowhere, but Jerrod was relieved. "All to myself. Daddy says that tomorrow we can go shopping and get some new toys. The fire ate mine." He seemed to be taking the fire better than Jerrod was. Maybe that was to be expected. He didn't understand the ramifications of losing nearly everything they had.

Chase said, "Maybe we can arrange for someone to get into the rooms at the back of the house so you can access some of what survived and get it out."

Jerrod shrugged. "That would be nice. I have no idea how long it's going to take before we can get access. I contacted the insurance company, and they said they would be sending someone out to try to help us." But he had no idea what they would be able to do. So far he had a billion questions with no answers, and the more he got, the more his anxiety grew.

"Petey," someone called, and Jerrod tensed at the familiar voice. He turned as Gizelle hurried through the restaurant, her dark hair askew and eyes wild. Peter stopped eating and looked at Jerrod, completely confused. "Don't you have a hug for your mommy?" she asked, standing next to his chair.

Peter didn't move, and Gizelle scowled.

"What are you doing here?" Jerrod asked. "I thought you moved to Baltimore." That had been a great day. The courts had terminated Gizelle's parental rights before Jerrod's brother passed away. She had been appealing that order for the past few years, and Jerrod hoped she never got anywhere.

"I decided to move back. I have friends here, and my son is here." Gizelle existed in a world of her own drama, and she picked and chose what she believed, which she seemed to feel gave her authority over everyone else. During her marriage to his brother, Gizelle had been just as likely to dote on Peter as she was to leave him alone for hours while she spent time at the neighbors'. It had been that chronic neglect and a lack of care that had caused the termination of her rights. More than once, Gizelle had put Peter in danger to the point others had had to intervene.

"Peter and I have had a very rough day." He tried to keep the anger out of his voice, but Gizelle was the last person either of them needed to see today. He glared at her, hoping she would simply leave.

"Can we help you?" Chase asked, his gaze not leaving Jerrod's. "We are trying to have dinner."

Gizelle glanced around. "I could join you."

"I don't think so." While Jerrod didn't talk ill of her in front of Peter, that didn't mean he wanted to have a meal with her. He glanced at Chase, who seemed a little lost. He did his best to send Chase messages. "Like I said, today has been difficult." He hoped she would take the hint, but she never had before.

She pursed her lips and set her shoulders like she was going to make a fuss. This was so not the time for any of Gizelle's dramatic antics.

Chase stood up, and Gizelle's gaze shifted to him, her eyes raking over him like he was a dinner buffet. He stepped away from the table, and Jerrod figured he was on his own. He didn't want her to make a big deal of things in front of Peter, who had settled back down to finish his dinner. He was about to just let her sit down when Chase returned with the hostess.

"We have the seat you requested in the bar," she told Gizelle. "If you'll follow me, please."

Gizelle seemed totally confused and completely taken off guard. Chase sat down and smiled as Gizelle had little choice but to follow the hostess to another part of the hotel. "Thank you," Jerrod said softly.

"Was that really my mom?" Peter asked. He hadn't seen her in a couple of years, and Jerrod had to agree that Gizelle hadn't been taking very good care of herself. She had changed quite a bit.

"Yes. It was."

"Oh," Peter said as he set down his spoon. "Does she love me?"

Jerrod found Chase watching him closely. "Yes, she does, in her own way. But your mom isn't able to take care of you, so that's why your papa asked me to look after you when he died." Thankfully, Peter seemed to accept that answer.

Chase was obviously curious about the rest of the story, and while there was plenty to tell, Jerrod wasn't going to say anything in front of Peter. He wanted Peter to keep whatever happy memories of his mother he had, rather than hear stories that would sour them.

"Do you have a mommy too?" Peter asked Chase.

"Yes. Mine lives in Arizona with my dad and sister. I see them a few times a year when they come to visit me or when I can go see them. It's a long way and takes a lot of time to get there." Peter nodded like he understood.

Jerrod finished up what he was eating, glancing occasionally at the door, worried that Gizelle would show up again.

"Can we go outside?" Peter asked.

"When you're done with your dinner," Jerrod answered before turning to Chase. "I need to let him run off some of his energy or he doesn't sleep very well." He ate the last of his food and took care of their check. He thought about paying for Chase's as well, but he already had his bill in hand, and dutch treat seemed to be the way to go. After all, this wasn't a date. Jerrod wouldn't mind if Chase asked him out sometime, though he figured that guy had probably had enough after the run-in with Gizelle.

After they paid their bills, Jerrod took Peter by the hand, and they left through the side exit to avoid the bar and Gizelle. To his surprise, Chase went along with them. "I live a few blocks that way," Chase offered. "There's a small back-lot park just over there."

"Can we go?" Peter asked.

"Sure," Jerrod answered. "Don't cross the street unless I'm with you," he said as Peter ran ahead. "He has so much energy sometimes. But I wouldn't change a thing."

"Is that really his mother in there?" Chase asked. "Why doesn't she have custody?"

"Gizelle basically abandoned Peter and my brother when Peter was about three. She went off for a couple months to God knows where and then came back like nothing had happened. Johnny took her back that first time, but she did it again, and this time she left Peter alone in the house. It was bad, and Johnny decided to divorce her. Gizelle fought for custody, but she lost." Jerrod noticed the disbelief in Chase's expression. "I know, it was a miracle in this state." He cautioned Peter to wait for them. "She got him on weekends, but she went off with her friends and left Peter locked in the house, asleep. Just left him. The only reason we found out was because Mom stopped by and found Peter alone. Johnny then petitioned to have her parental rights terminated, and when Gizelle disappeared one more time, the petition was granted." It was so sad. "I can't figure out how she could do any of that. Johnny died in an accident two years ago, and he named me guardian of Peter. Now Gizelle shows up occasionally, and she's appealing the termination order." Sometimes it seemed it would never end. Apparently with her appeals, he didn't have to do anything, but he always responded to make sure the court knew his position.

"And after all that…." Chase paused at the corner, where they caught up with Peter. The three of them crossed the street, and Peter raced ahead again and then back before skipping up ahead once more. "I take it Peter has no idea."

"No. I don't want him to think his mother abandoned him. He hadn't seen her in a long time, and it's likely she'll disappear again." God, he hoped so. "I never tell her anything about our lives or where we live. Basically she's a stranger to Peter, and I think that's best."

Chase stopped on the sidewalk. "You're one hell of a man. That's all I can say."

Jerrod's eyes grew warm, and Chase licked his lips as their gazes met. For a second he thought Chase might lean closer and try to kiss him. Just the idea had Jerrod's pulse racing and raised the summer evening temperature to scorching.

"Daddy, are we close to the park?" Peter asked, and the moment popped like a soap bubble. Jerrod blinked, and Chase turned away. "Mr. Fireman, are we almost there?"

"Just a few more blocks," Chase answered, his voice rough. Then they began walking again. Jerrod would have wondered if it had all been his imagination except for the hitch in that deep voice. Chase cleared his throat, and Jerrod held out his hand. Peter took it, and the three of them continued on to the park, with Jerrod's head spinning slightly the entire way.

CHAPTER 3

"CAN WE go back to the scene of that fire on Walnut?" Chase asked Hayden the following morning.

"Why? I already filed my report on that fire." He sipped his coffee as though nothing was wrong, but the more Chase thought about it, the more certain he became that Hayden had missed something. He took a deep breath and held it because his instinct was to blurt out that he wanted to go because Hayden was wrong about the electrical cause. "It was electrical, pure and simple." The stubbornness in his voice told Chase that he was going to get nowhere. "What's wrong? You look like hell."

"Gee, thanks," Chase muttered. "I didn't sleep very well. Everything is new, and I guess it's going to take some getting used to." That was bullshit. He kept seeing big brown eyes and full lips every time he closed his eyes, and he knew that once Hayden filed his report, there was going to be fallout. An electrician's house burning down because of an electrical fire was as bad as a fire at a firefighter's home. It did not instill confidence.

He poured a mug of coffee to try to wake himself up, but an incoming call to the scene of an accident on the freeway had a more immediate effect. Chase set down his mug and his training kicked in.

It took less than five minutes for them to arrive on the scene. They sprang into action, extricating people from cars and getting them to the arriving ambulances. Thankfully, there was no fire, and as soon as the victims were cared for, they packed up and returned to the station. Chase jumped down from the truck, then stowed his gear where it belonged for quick retrieval. He hoped he'd get a chance to return to his coffee, but the captain corralled him and Hayden as soon as they returned.

"I need to see you in my office," he said as he passed, striding to the printer. "Now." The snap in his voice left no doubt about the urgency.

Chase was the first to arrive, surprised that Jerrod was already inside.

"Is Peter okay?" Chase asked with a slight smile.

"You were part of the investigation?" Jerrod asked, his eyes stone cold and filled with anger.

"Chase took part for educational purposes," the captain explained. "Hayden was the lead investigator," he added once Hayden came in. The captain turned to him. "I want you to understand that I am not asking or requiring either of you to change your report for the fire on Walnut."

Hayden crossed his arms over his chest. "Good." He sounded a little like he was being a dick. "Because that wouldn't be right."

Jerrod stood tall, glaring at Hayden. "I know there was nothing wrong with that electrical work. I rewired the house myself, and I have the borough inspection report to prove it. There is no way that fire could have started there."

"I know what I saw. The box was fried beyond belief," Hayden said. "It had to start there."

Chase cleared his throat, looking at Hayden and then at the captain. He didn't dare glance at Jerrod. "I don't agree with Hayden's conclusions. I think the fire started in that vicinity in the basement, but I think there may be another cause." Damn, he was destroying his relationship with one of the senior firefighters. He might as well start looking for another job. "I don't know for sure, but something has been bothering me." He figured it was time to back off.

"All right. We owe it to the department and to the people we're here to protect and serve to make sure we're right." The captain looked at Jerrod. "I have experience in this area as well, so the three of us are going to return to that fire scene and have a second look. If we need to amend the report, we will do so."

"I want to be there," Jerrod said.

"Agreed. But you will not enter the building without our permission, and you'll be there only if we have questions," the captain said. "Now, get your gear together and we'll leave in ten." He lowered his gaze to the desk, and Chase followed Hayden out the door.

"Why are you doing this to me?" Jerrod asked Hayden once they reached the station common room.

"I'm just doing my job. I can't let the fact that you're a friend of Chase's affect my judgment. I had to include what I thought in the report, regardless of that friendship." The way Hayden looked at Chase told him there was very little "friendship" there.

"Okay, I'll give you that, but you didn't need to go out of your way to find something that will ruin me," Jerrod said. "I know you think—"

"Get ready to go," the captain said as he came out of his office.

Chase got his gear and hurried to the truck, then climbed in to ride with the captain, grateful that Hayden was taking another vehicle. He didn't talk as he rode, a little intimidated about being in the cab with the captain and kicking himself for opening his big mouth. Sometimes being right came at a cost. Chase had no idea what the fallout was going to be, whether he was right or not.

"I expect all the people I work with to be professional, and that means accepting that others may have a different opinion," the captain told him. "Speaking up was the right thing to do."

"Thanks," Chase said.

They pulled to a stop in front of the shell of what had once been Jerrod's home. He climbed out, and Hayden pulled up behind them.

"The stairs down are around the back."

Jerrod pulled up and got out of his car. Chase waved briefly before leading their group around the side of the building to the back door. The firefighters went inside and down the stairs, careful of their steps, leaving Jerrod waiting outside.

"Where is the box?"

"There." Hayden pointed. "Right near the hole in the floor." He went on to explain his logic and how he thought the fire had behaved. The captain nodded, and Chase began to doubt himself.

"What makes you question Hayden's conclusion?" the captain asked.

"The hole in the floor isn't in the right place. Why burn through there rather than right above the electrical box? I understand that could have been the weakest spot, but look at this." He knelt down.

"That's just debris," Hayden said. "I told you that before."

The captain joined him. "These look like electrical caps that have melted." He pulled out an extendable poker and worked through the pile of charred remains. "Here's another one and a few bits of wire." He looked closer and then at Hayden before continuing to work through the debris. Then he stood to get closer to the charred beams without touching them. "There are no wires running through this section of the floor. They run toward the front and back of the house, but not directly across here." He checked around more closely and then stood. "This fire may have started electrically, but it wasn't at the electrical panel—though it's my belief it was made to seem that way."

"Captain?" Chase asked as what he was saying sank into his head.

"Yeah. This fire wasn't an accident. It was arson. Someone set this fire and tried to make it seem like an electrical issue, probably to destroy Mr. Whipkey's house and ruin his reputation at the same time." He collapsed his poker and slipped it into his pocket, looking at Hayden. Chase pulled out his phone and began taking pictures for evidence, being sure to highlight everything they had found. The police would need to send someone out to gather evidence, and Chase hoped that pictures would help.

"I see," Hayden said, growing surly.

"Stop," the captain said. "None of us get it right all the time. Fire is sometimes an unpredictable beast, and even the best of us make mistakes." He sighed. "What I need you to do is rewrite your report to reflect our new findings and then get it to me by the end of the day so I can forward a copy to the police. If this was arson, then someone burned down this home deliberately, and we're going to need their help to find who it was."

Hayden paled slightly as he nodded. "I'll make sure it gets done," he said softly, and they all headed for the stairs.

Chase was relieved and keyed up at the same time as the captain strode to where Jerrod paced along the sidewalk. "What did you find?"

"We no longer believe the fire was started by the electrical work in the house. It seems that someone started the fire, trying to make it appear that way. We found bits of electrical wire and caps on the floor, away from the box."

Jerrod sighed. "Okay. That's good news. At least no one can think it's my fault. Wait… are you saying what I think you are?" He paled.

"I'm afraid so. Rather than being an accident, it seems that the fire in your home was set deliberately. We will be forwarding our findings to the police, and I'm sure they will be in touch with you."

Jerrod blinked and began to sway on his feet. Chase caught him before he could go down and helped him to the truck, where he sat him on the seat. "Someone tried to kill me and Peter?" He blinked. "Who would want to hurt my son?" He began to shake.

"We don't know. But we'll be here to try to help figure it out," Hayden said. All traces of the dick he'd been earlier had vanished.

"Yeah… okay." Jerrod took a deep breath. "Sorry. I'm okay now. What the hell am I going to do? How do I keep Peter safe? There's someone out there willing to burn down my house, and I have no idea who they are."

"That's why the police are going to get involved. They have to help figure out who did this. They also have access to the crime labs to have the things we found in the basement tested. But I'm afraid this is going to send your insurance company into a tailspin, because they aren't going to pay out until they know you aren't involved."

Jerrod groaned. "Of course. They're going to put off paying the claim for as long as possible. But at least there aren't going to be rumors running through town that I burned down my own house because of bad wiring. I'd never be able to get another job." He seemed to be calming down, but Chase couldn't blame him for being upset. If he thought someone was after him, he had no idea how he'd react.

"Where is Peter now?" Chase asked.

"At day care."

"Then I suggest you contact them and let them know that there is a possible threat to your son so they can help keep him safe," the captain said.

Judging by the way Jerrod bit his lower lip, that did nothing to reassure him. "They can help when he's at school, but what about the hotel? Anyone can come and go there. Security is nonexistent. Hell, the elevators are in the lobby, and that's open to the public because of the restaurant. They don't even require a key to access the upper floors." He sounded even more nervous now.

Chase wanted to help but wasn't sure how. "Thanks, Captain," he ended up saying. "Why don't you follow us back to the station and we'll try to figure out something," Chase offered.

Jerrod nodded and stood up again, his legs steadier. Chase watched Jerrod until he got into his truck and then joined the captain, pulling the passenger door closed while Hayden got in his truck. That seemed to be the signal for the start of the inquisition.

"What do you think we can do?" the captain asked. "We aren't a social agency, and while we found evidence of arson, for all we know, he could have set the fire himself."

Chase tried to stop his mouth from gaping open like a fish. "Do you really think that? You saw him. He's panicked, and he has a kid—the one I rescued from that fire. I saw his relief and fear—they were real. And if he set the fire, then why complain about Hayden's findings in the first place?"

Captain Greg sighed. "Then what do you have in mind? I don't have the resources to give them security, and the borough police don't either."

Chase shrugged as he tried to think of options and came up empty. "I don't know. But Peter could have died in that fire." He refused to let the captain see him shiver like some little kid at a Dracula marathon, but that was how he felt at the moment. "I have a one-bedroom apartment...."

"No way. You can't let yourself get dragged into the dealings of every person we help. That isn't going to end well. It's unprofessional and a recipe for disaster." He pulled to a stop at a light. "You don't know this man at all, and while I understand wanting to help...." He gripped the steering wheel tightly.

"So we just leave them in trouble. Is that who we are?"

The captain continued forward. "Look, I know a few people in town that might be able to help. They have a few buildings with apartments. I don't know if there are vacancies, but I can see. But if someone tried to burn them out again, we'd be in a heap of hurt, and it's going to be my ass." He shook his head. "I swore I'd never ask my fucking brother-in-law for anything," he muttered under his breath.

"Thanks."

"Don't thank me yet. It's going to be your responsibility to make sure my brother-in-law's building isn't next, or so help me, I'll make you explain it to my wife. And let me tell you, I love her to death, but you do not want to see her angry." He pulled into the station. "At least we'll have done our good deed for the week—maybe the month—with this one." He parked in the lot, and they got out. The captain strode into the station while Chase held back, waiting for Hayden.

"Hay, I didn't mean to show you up," Chase said when Hayden got out of his truck.

"No, I should have listened to you the first time." He clapped Chase on the shoulder. "My partner, Kyle, is always telling me that I need to listen more and talk less. I went for the easiest answer, but I should have ruled out anything else before drawing a conclusion."

They went inside together, and then Chase headed to the trucks to see what needed to be done while Hayden most likely went to revise his report. Paperwork was the bane of everyone's existence, and a firefighter was no exception.

The crew had everything in hand, so Chase found Jerrod outside the captain's office. He sat in the plastic molded chair next to him. "He's going to see if he can pull a few strings, maybe find you and Peter a more permanent place to stay."

"I don't know how to thank you."

"Well, don't yet. He hasn't done anything other than agree to make a few phone calls." He leaned forward. "Look, the police are going to ask you who might want to do this to you."

"You met one of them last night. Peter's mother isn't the most stable person. But I don't see her as able to keep a secret. If she had known about the fire in any way, she would have tried to use it as leverage. She didn't. Gizelle is manipulative and self-serving above all else."

Chase nodded. "I got that from her, but we still can't rule her out. Manipulative people often have traits we aren't aware of until they decide to show them. Who else? Since there were electrical supplies used, could one of the guys you had to let go decide to try to get even?"

Jerrod shrugged. "I don't know. Maybe. But who burns down someone's home for pulling someone off a job? Neither of them were good electricians, and I can't have been the only one to let them go. What are they going to do, set fire to everyone who decides not to work with them? I just don't have any idea who would want to do this to me."

"I get that. No one wants to think that someone would hate them that much." The most important thing at the moment was to find a place where Jerrod and Peter could be safe. Once that was done, Chase could get his mind around this mystery.

He shook his head. What the hell was he doing? He was a rookie firefighter, not a trained investigator. The police needed to take it from here… and yet the thought of Jerrod leaving the station and Chase never seeing him again left him cold and wondering what he'd be missing out on.

CHAPTER 4

"YOU SHOULDN'T have to help me find somewhere to stay," Jerrod said. The near panic from earlier had subsided, and he was starting to think straight again. Yes, he needed a place to stay that wasn't a hotel and somewhere that he could keep Peter safe, but....

Chase leaned closer, a wry smile making his eyes twinkle. "The captain is calling in a favor from his brother-in-law. I think he would rather have oral surgery, but he's making the call."

"Why would he do that?" Jerrod watched as Chase's expression fell, and he realized it was because Chase had asked him to. "You don't need to go out on a limb for me." Still, he was honored and grateful. It had been a while since anyone had stood up for him. Not since Johnny.

As a kid, Jerrod had been scrawny and small, therefore a target for bullies who had something to prove. Johnny was two years ahead of him, and when they were in the same school, he always looked out for Jerrod. When the bullies came calling, they found out the price for bullying him. Thankfully that changed when Jerrod reached puberty and he caught up to the other kids, but Johnny was always there, encouraging him. Johnny had been whip smart, Jerrod not so much. But Johnny had encouraged him to find something he was good at and to go for it. Sometimes he still heard his older brother's voice in his head, encouraging him, telling him he could do it.

"I didn't. The captain is a really good guy, and he knows what you're going through." Chase stood, and Jerrod let his gaze rake over him. The man was fine in the most amazing sense of the word. Broad shoulders, narrow waist, incredible eyes, and a mop of hair that seemed to have a mind of its own, but only managed to make Chase look rakish.

"I appreciate it very much." Jerrod leaned back in the chair, finally letting go of some of his tension, but when an alarm went off, he jumped to his feet, wondering what the hell was going on.

"I have to go," Chase said as the other firefighters hurried through the station. The captain popped out of his office and shoved a piece of paper into Jerrod's hand as he raced past. Soon sirens sounded as the trucks pulled out, and Jerrod found himself in a largely empty station with just a few of the crew staying behind. Not knowing what else to do, he looked at the paper, which listed a name and a phone number, and then he headed back to his truck.

Jerrod clutched the piece of paper like a lifeline. He hadn't expected anything to come from stopping by the station, and now he was shocked and pleased. At least he might have a line on a place to live. He had been making calls for the past few days, only to find that many of the places listed in ads had already been taken and that Carlisle had a drought of available rental units.

Though it seemed that when the resolution to one possible situation appeared, another reared its ugly head. Someone had deliberately set fire to his home. That alone made the air whoosh out of his lungs.

He climbed into the truck and sat in the driver's seat, staring out the window without seeing anything. He had nearly lost Peter in that fire, and now he was homeless and at the mercy of the insurance company, which was certain to use the investigation as a chance to delay paying any claims. Jerrod took a deep breath and wondered who might have done such a thing. He didn't go around making enemies. He was an electrician who helped people build their homes. He worked on condos and on private homes. He wasn't some bigwig who decided who worked and who didn't; he was just a guy trying to make a living.

Jerrod's phone rang, and he answered it and confirmed to the client that he was on the way and would be there soon. Starting the engine, he pushed aside all the thoughts racing through his head and tried to get back to work.

WORK HAD always taken his complete concentration. He needed to make sure all his work was up to code and that he made all the connections correctly. People paid quite a bit for his expertise, and it was up to him to make sure they got their money's worth.

"Everything is done, and your kitchen wiring is now correct," he told the hunched lady leaning on her cane as he presented her with the bill. The lights in her kitchen had taken to flickering on and off at unusual times. At first he thought it had been the switches, and they had been bad, but the wiring itself had needed to be replaced. Some of it had been installed in the twenties, and the cloth wrapping had worn away. Jerrod demonstrated all the switches and outlets, showing her that they worked each and every time.

"Thank you for helping. I wasn't sure what to do and was afraid of a fire in the walls."

Jerrod had to suppress a shudder. "You're welcome," he said gently. "I'm glad I could help."

She went to the table and wrote him a check. Jerrod thanked her again before picking up his toolbox and returning to his truck. After stowing everything, he sat in front of the house and pulled out the piece of paper from earlier to make the call.

"I'm Jerrod, and I was told you might have a temporary apartment for me and my son," Jerrod explained. "The captain at the fire station gave me the number."

"Yes, I might," the man said gruffly. "Look, I don't rent to transients or people with credit problems. My place doesn't have a revolving door."

"Well, my home burned down, and I'm looking for a place to stay while the insurance people do their thing and I can figure out if I can rebuild or need to buy a new place. Mainly I need to have a place for my son to live instead of a hotel. The guys at the fire station were good enough to try to help."

"Okay." The man gave Jerrod the address on Louther Street.

"I just finished work, and I can stop by when it's convenient for you."

A heavy sigh followed. "I'll be there in ten minutes." A click told him that the call had ended. Jerrod couldn't help wondering what he had gotten in the middle of, but he pulled away and drove to where he'd been instructed. When he stopped, he wasn't sure if he had the right place. Still, he got out, looking up and down the street.

"You Jerrod?" a man asked, popping his head out of the door at the address specified. "I'm Kyle. My dad said to show you the rental." He opened the door, and Jerrod went inside. "You know Uncle Greg?"

"The captain? I met him at the station. Our home burned, and I need a place for me and my son."

Kyle nodded. "This is the living room. The kitchen and dining room are through there." The rooms were small but clean, with fresh paint. "There's two bedrooms and a bath upstairs."

"I didn't realize the rental was the entire house."

Kyle shrugged. "Uncle Greg said you needed a place right away, and this is what we have available. Dad and Mom have almost twenty units in town. Dad was just going to advertise this one when Uncle Greg called. So this is what we've got. It's a nice place. My grandparents lived here before they died, and Dad kept it as a rental." He followed Jerrod upstairs.

The bedrooms were in the same shape as the downstairs, clean, basic, but nicer that he had expected. There was room for Peter, and there was a yard out back with a swing set for him to play on.

This was what they truly needed. "What comes with it? The only reason I'm asking is because we lost everything in the fire and—"

"The appliances are here, and they all work." He smiled and shrugged. "There isn't much else. You'll need to get furniture and stuff." He went on to explain the rent, payments, and due dates. "We'd like a six-month lease to begin with. Dad usually does a year, but with your situation, we'll do six months, if that helps." He smiled, and Jerrod smiled back.

"That would help a lot. Thank you." He was already trying to sort through how he could make this work financially. He figured he would need to contact the insurance company and see what they were going to do. After all, even though the house had burned, he was still responsible for all the other things that went along with owning a house. Most of that would continue regardless of the state of the property.

"So you'll take it?"

"Yes. It's a nice place," Jerrod said. "Tell your father I appreciate his help."

Kyle nodded slowly. "I'll tell Dad to get the lease written up so you can sign it, and then you can move yourself in and stuff." He led the way to the front door. "I think Dad said you were an electrician."

"Yeah. I have my own business."

"Cool. I'll let Dad know. We often need work like that done when he buys a new place." He shook Jerrod's hand, and they left the house, with Kyle locking up. "I'll call you once we have the lease done, probably today, and we'll get it signed so you can move in."

"Thanks."

Kyle nodded and turned, walking down the block toward one of the brick row homes. He went inside, and Jerrod got in his truck. One problem solved. He had a place for Peter and himself to live. Now he needed to talk to the insurance company to find out what help they could provide. But the big questions remained, and he had no idea how he was going to get answers.

"Are we leaving, Daddy?" Peter asked as Jerrod finished packing up the few things they had at the hotel.

"Yes. I found us a place to live, and we're going there." He had managed to get a bed for Peter and a few pieces of furniture. The insurance company had agreed to help, but only on a limited basis until the questions around the cause of the fire and who was involved were answered. The fact that the police and the fire department didn't think he was involved helped, but the insurance company had decided to perform their own investigation, which probably meant they were stalling for time before paying. Still, he was getting them into a more permanent home.

"Will I have my own bed?" Peter asked.

"Yes. I already have it set up in your room."

"What about my toys? Are they there too?" Peter asked.

"A few of them." Jerrod sat on the edge of the bed. "A lot of them were burned up in the house." They had lost so much. Jerrod lifted Peter onto his lap. "I'll see if I can go into the house and get what's still there, but I don't know when they'll let me." He hoped it would be soon. "But I'll do my best to get you new toys and stuff."

Peter looked up at him, his eyes wide. "Is the fireman going to be with us?"

Jerrod paused. "No. Why, do you think he should?"

"Who will save me if the house catches fire again?" he asked as though it were a completely logical supposition.

Jerrod pulled Peter into a hug. "That isn't going to happen again." At least he hoped not.

"Are you sure? Do you promise? I don't want to be burned. Maybe you should call the fireman and make sure he keeps us safe."

Jerrod chuckled. "Chase. The fireman's name was Chase, and he helped us get the house we're going to move into."

"But what if it goes on fire?" he asked again. "I'm scared, Daddy." He hugged Jerrod tighter, and they sat together on the side of the bed, comforting each other.

"I know, buddy. But I'm going to do everything I can to keep you safe. The house is nice, and the people who we're going to be renting it from live down the street. Everyone wants us to be safe, including the firefighters." God, the last thing he wanted was to see Peter being pulled out of another building. He had nightmares about Peter every night, and he woke up in a cold sweat after not getting to him in time.

"It's going to be you and me, and we're going to watch out for each other." He hugged Peter once more before carefully setting him back on his feet. "Let's finish packing so you can see the new house and your new room." There had to be something he could get Peter excited about.

"Okay." Peter rushed to the bathroom and returned with all the hotel towels in his arms.

"What are you doing?"

"The old ones burned, so we need new ones." He set the load on the bed and raced back, then returned with more that he added to the pile.

"Those aren't ours. We have to leave them here," Jerrod said gently, closing his suitcase, and then he began putting everything back. "We'll have to buy our own towels and stuff." Once he was done and their possessions, meager as they were, had been packed, he took Peter's hand and led the way out of the room and down the hall to the elevator.

It took a few minutes to check out, and then they were on their way to the house. "Who is that?" Peter asked as someone came out of their rental.

"Chase?" Jerrod asked as he pulled to a stop. "What are you doing here?"

"The team took up a collection of sorts. It isn't much, but Hayden had a chair he wasn't using anymore, and some of the others had things. I gathered them and brought them over. I know it isn't a lot, but we figured that you'd need most everything."

Jerrod went inside.

The living room had boxes stacked against one wall. A chair and a coffee table sat in the center of the room. "What's all this?" He was more than a little taken aback.

"Many of the firefighters' families have things they no longer use. One of the boxes has pans and some kitchen things. There are some basic appliances and silverware. There are some mismatched towels, but they're clean—I put them through a cycle in the station laundry. Just things we knew you had lost and were going to need."

Jerrod didn't know what to say. "And you brought it all over?"

"It was just a truckload. There's also a bedframe, but you'll need to get your own mattress." Peter raced past them, through the room and up the stairs, his footsteps echoing through the largely empty house.

"Daddy!" This cry was one of delight and excitement. Then footsteps approached the stairs and he barreled down and into Jerrod's arms. "There are toys. My toys." He jumped up and down for a few seconds before hurrying back upstairs.

"I was able to get in the house and brought out a few bags of things from upstairs. I put the cleaned toys I could save into Peter's room, and the bags in the other bedroom are what I could get of the things that seemed to be yours. His room was less burned, so there isn't much of your stuff, but I brought what I could. We'll have to wash everything."

"I was going to ask if I could go inside," Jerrod said.

"The police are still investigating, so it's off-limits. But they let me in once I explained what I was looking for and promised not to go to the basement or the main floor."

"Thank you." He didn't know what else to say. No one had gone as far as this man to help him, and Chase was largely a stranger. "I really appreciate the help." He'd go through the stuff later. "I'd offer you something to drink, but…." He shrugged and looked around.

"Daddy, can we have pizza? I'm hungry," Peter called as he came back down the stairs with his favorite stuffed turtle under his arm. "Look what I found. I thought he was lost forever." Peter cradled the toy, rocking back and forth. "Maybe he's a super turtle that can't be burned up."

It felt so good to see Peter smile that it made Jerrod's heart ache. "What else was there?"

"All my Legos and my army men. The fireman brought them all!" He was so excited. "And there are dinosaurs. Roarrrr…." He ran back up the stairs.

"There are also fresh sheets for both of you in the boxes. I washed them as well." Chase flashed that smile, and Jerrod had no idea what to do. This was too much, and yet he didn't have the strength to turn anything down. He and Peter were starting over from scratch—less than scratch, because Johnny's pictures of Peter had been in the house as well. "I can't imagine how hard all of this is, but we hoped this would help."

"It does. Please thank everyone for their generosity and thoughtfulness." All he wanted to do was go somewhere, be alone, and lick what felt like mortal wounds. Instead, he found himself standing in a strange living room, shaking like a leaf. "Sorry." He fought to get himself under control and nearly had it when he found himself wrapped in a pair of strong arms holding him tightly.

"It's okay. Everything is going to work out in the end," Chase said softly. "I know you probably feel like it, but you aren't alone."

Jerrod closed his eyes, trying very hard not to need the comfort Chase offered so easily, but he really did.

"Daddy, I want a hug too," Peter said as he hurried into the room. Chase backed away and lifted Peter, then gently hugged them both. It was as strange and comforting as anything Jerrod could remember.

CHAPTER 5

"CAN THE fireman stay?" Peter asked after a few seconds.

Chase chuckled as he backed away, feeling like a fool and hoping his forwardness wasn't out of line. He'd just felt like Jerrod needed some sort of comfort. Chase had wanted to kiss the man into complete mindlessness, but he'd hugged him instead.

"He probably needs to go back to work."

"But what if this house burns down? We need the fireman here to save us." Peter was so serious, his eyes filled with fear.

"Your daddy has my phone number, and if that happens, we'll be here right away," Chase said, trying to be polite. They didn't need him butting in. "But everything is going to be okay." He knelt down. "I know it seems scary after what happened, but your daddy is going to keep you safe." He lifted his gaze to Jerrod. "And I'm your friend, and I'll be watching out too. I promise. Okay?"

Peter nodded and then hurried away, back up the stairs.

"I don't know what to tell him. Whoever set fire to our house is out there, and what if they try something here? I keep wondering what I'm going to do. I put Peter in the back bedroom, and I already know the ways to get him out of the house if something does happen. But living in fear is terrible."

"Okay, then let's talk about it," Chase said. "The best way to end this is to figure out who could have done this." He lifted one of the kitchen boxes and carried it into the other room.

"You've already done enough," Jerrod said as he grabbed another box. This one said it contained pans. He opened it and began putting the cookware into a lower cupboard near the stove.

"Where do the dishes go?" Chase asked, then began putting them in the cupboard Jerrod picked near the sink. It seemed his plans to leave had been hijacked. Not that he really minded. "Okay. We already have Gizelle on the list. What were the names of the two guys you let go?"

"Steve and Gary. I don't remember their last names offhand," Jerrod answered.

Chase pulled out a small tablet from his pocket and took down the information.

"They both live here in Carlisle as far as I know. They could have moved away, but I don't know for sure. I saw Steve in town a few weeks ago."

Chase put the tablet back in his pocket. "All right. Who else might wish you ill?"

Jerrod set the empty box in the corner and retrieved another. "I don't know. I had a client who gave me trouble, but we worked everything out. I'm just an electrician."

"All right. There is the possibility that the guy who did this is a firebug and likes to watch things burn. That could also be it." Chase was offering possibilities, but even as he said it, it didn't seem to fit.

Jerrod pulled open a drawer and paused. "It seems really personal to me. Maybe it's because it was my house, but...."

"I thought so too." Someone went to a lot of trouble to try to make it seem like the wiring was the issue. That seemed very personal and close to home. Someone really wanted to hurt Jerrod, and the thought had Chase clenching a fist without even realizing it. "So if that's the case, then who might have done it? Gizelle doesn't seem like the type, and arson is overwhelmingly a male crime. Doesn't mean it couldn't have been her, though." He put away the glasses as he continued thinking. "You know, it could be some kind of rival."

Jerrod reached over the stove to put something away, the hem of his shirt riding up just enough to give Chase a glimpse of a band of golden skin, and he forgot his train of thought for a few seconds. Damn, Jerrod was gorgeous.

"I don't have rivals, not like that. Sure, I beat guys out of jobs, and sometimes others beat me—it's the name of the game. I have a large job set to start in a couple weeks that's going to keep me busy for almost a year. Those new condos out north of town. I got a subcontract to wire them. I have a couple guys I've worked with before to do it with me. The three of us formed a partnership to bid on the work. It should be a really good job."

"Then who did you beat out?" Chase asked, breaking down the empty boxes. "If it's going to be lucrative for you, then you took that peach job away from someone else."

Jerrod shrugged. "It was a sealed bid. We put in our bid, and others did the same. It was as simple as that. Because the three of us are nimble and don't have huge overhead, we were able to come in at a good price." He paused, blinking a few times.

"And if the fire at your house had been declared electrical in origin…?" Chase posed.

"Then the overall contractor might have wanted to rethink the deal," Jerrod said before swearing under his breath. "But I have no way of knowing who the other bidders were, and the general contractor can't reveal them."

"No. That's something we can point the police toward, though. Maybe they can gain access." Chase jotted that down. Hayden would probably have a few contacts with the borough police that they could pass the information on to.

"Okay. That makes sense," Jerrod said. "And if that's true, them going after me here makes no sense, because I haven't worked on this house." He seemed to breathe a sigh of relief. "Starting a fire here won't get them anywhere."

"That's true."

"And I always pull permits and have my work inspected. That isn't foolproof, but it does mean that my work has been gone over by a second set of eyes. If I was trying to work under the table, I'd be a lot more vulnerable."

"Can't argue with that," Chase agreed, returning to the living room. "Let's get these boxes upstairs where you're going to need them." He hefted the first one and headed for the stairs. Jerrod followed him. Chase put the box of towels and stuff in the bathroom and returned for the bags of things he thought were Jerrod's, which he placed in the largely empty bedroom. "Where had you intended to sleep?"

"I haven't had a chance to think about it much. Mostly I've been worried about Peter. I got him a bed, but I figured I could sleep on the floor for now." He stood in the center of the room, looking kind of lost. "I guess I should get myself over to one of the mattress stores and figure something out. I'm also going to need a sofa and a few lamps and stuff."

"And probably a television," Chase said.

Jerrod shrugged. "Eventually, though that isn't a really high priority. Peter and I don't watch a lot. I read to him every night, and we play games together when we're home. I'm going to need to go out and replace some of the ones he really likes."

"That's cool," Chase said.

"I grew up spending hours in front of the TV watching just about anything that was on. I don't want Peter to do that. I had an iPad in the house, but I limited Peter's screen time. I don't want him to disappear behind one of those. When the evenings were nice, we'd go out for a walk to one of the parks where he could play."

"I have to give you a lot of credit. It would be so much easier to let the TV act as a babysitter," Chase said.

"My mom did that a lot. Johnny always said he wanted better for Peter, so I'm trying to live up to his wishes." Jerrod nodded, almost to himself. "I have no idea why I'm telling you all this. It must be boring as heck."

Chase actually smiled. "It sounds like you're trying to give Peter the best childhood you can." His parents had cared for him, and Chase knew he was loved, but only up to a point. "Was it just you and your brother?"

"Yes. And it was so hard on everyone when he died. He was like the perfect son and older brother. Not that Mom and Dad ever said anything. He was the oldest, and he watched out for me and helped keep me out of trouble." Jerrod leaned against the door frame. "I was in seventh grade when Johnny caught me behind the garage smoking a cigarette. It was embarrassing how stupid I was. He snatched the cigarette away and glared at me before passing it back, making me smoke the rest of it and then what was left of the pack, one after the other. I got so sick and coughed so much I swore I was going to pass out. To this day, I can't stand the smell of cigarettes. And as far as I know, he never told Mom or Dad. That was the end of it." He sighed. "What about you?"

"I have a younger sister. She's sixteen and still lives with my parents. Mom didn't think she could have kids after me, and then eight years later, she had Julie." Chase shrugged. "She's completely spoiled and gets away with anything she wants. I was glad when Mom and Dad moved away. They bought their retirement home in the Southwest and took Julie with them."

"You don't like her?" Jerrod asked.

"I don't know her all that well. I left for school six years ago when she was ten. When I went to high school, she was six, so we don't have much in common, and we're at very different points in our lives. I see her just a few times a year, and lately she's always been really busy, so I guess what I hear is what Mom and Dad tell me." He knew that was skewed because Julie was a teenager, and that was a rough time for everyone in the family. He turned to look down the hallway as Peter came out of his room, barreling toward them. The kid seemed to have one speed: zoom.

"Hey, buddy. Do you like your new room?"

"Yes," he answered. "Daddy, did you forget the pizza? My tummy is really hungry. It's making noises."

"I did. I'm sorry. What kind do you want?"

"Cheese and pepperponies," Peter answered, and Jerrod nodded and placed an order to be delivered. He also got some drinks and asked Chase what he wanted. Chase had never been picky about that sort of thing, so Jerrod got a half pepperoni and half everything pizza before ending the call.

"Can your tummy wait twenty minutes, or does it need a cracker?"

Peter seemed to listen. "It says it needs twooooo crackers."

"Oh, it does?" Jerrod swept Peter into the air to giggles that filled the largely empty room with happiness. "Let's go downstairs and get you those crackers." He flew Peter around the room and then out the door, and carried him down the stairs, leaving laughter in their wake. Chase followed, carted along by the sound and the carefree smile on Jerrod's face.

"I should get going," Chase said when he joined the happy family of two in the living room.

"Please stay. I ordered plenty of pizza, and it's the least I can do after all you've done for us." He handed Peter two crackers from a package out of a Giant grocery bag and carried it to the kitchen.

"Are you sure?" Chase asked. He didn't want to impose.

Jerrod paused as he put the groceries away, turning back to him. "If it weren't for you, I'd be fighting for my career, still looking for a place to live, and trying to scrounge up even the most basic things for Peter and me." He drew closer, and Chase's heart skipped a beat. "I didn't even know you before our lives fell apart, and you've done more for me than anyone has in a long time." Those eyes grew deeper by the second. "I can't thank you enough for any of it." He leaned against the counter. "Where did you come from?"

"Excuse me?" Chase asked.

"Are you, like, some angel in hot fireman form? Is that what's happening?" His voice lowered to just above a whisper.

Chase smiled. "You think I'm hot?"

Jerrod rolled his eyes dramatically. "That's all you took from everything I said?" For a few seconds he looked like a mischievous boy. "I opened up about all the things you've done, and all you heard was that I think you're hot."

"Every guy likes to think he's hot," Chase said with a grin, inordinately pleased that Jerrod thought him attractive. "And you're welcome. I know it's hard trying to start a life, but I can't imagine having to start over from scratch." Hell, there was so much more than that. Losing your home meant finding a new one, not just rebuilding a life from scratch, but losing pieces of your history, things that couldn't be replaced. "I'm just glad that I was able to help."

"You've done a great deal." The bell rang, and Peter hurried over to the door, jumping with excitement as Jerrod retrieved the pizza and soda. He tipped the delivery man and then thanked him before closing the door. "Who's hungry?"

"Me. I'm starving," Peter said dramatically as Jerrod set down the box and got a plate, then gave Peter a slice of his pizza. He also got him a glass and settled on the floor at the coffee table to eat. Jerrod took a slice of the everything, with Chase following behind him, his stomach growling at the enticing scent.

"Are you off today?" Jerrod asked between bites.

"Yes," Chase answered, then took a bite, loving the unctuous sauce and tangy cheese. This was what a pizza should be. "The shift lengths vary, so I'm off for a few days, actually. I don't have to be back at the station until Thursday. When you're there, you're always ready for action. It creates a certain tension that doesn't go away until you've got a few days off. At least that's what Hayden tells me."

Jerrod nodded. "Have any of your coworkers given you a tough time?"

Firefighting was a tough profession, with the teams living in close quarters sometimes. "A few of the men have kept their distance. Hayden says not to worry and that they'll come around in time. I'm not so sure, but there hasn't been any outright harassment or anything. The captain is pretty vocal about that kind of stuff." Still, he had expected some pushback. Then again, maybe Hayden having already tested those waters ensured that there would be fewer issues for him. "There is a couple at the fire station downtown. Apparently they're married now. I haven't met them yet, but they're sort of famous around the department for pulling off an effort to save their existing station from being turned into a museum and moved to a new location. They raised a lot of money to upgrade the station, and the borough stepped in to renovate part of it because of the publicity."

Jerrod nodded and swallowed. "That's really impressive. So, I was going to take Peter to the park this afternoon and wondered if you might want to come with us. They finally finished the new play area."

"That would be nice. Thanks." Chase was about to take another bite when his phone vibrated. He checked it and acknowledged the message. "I have to go. I'm being called in." He hurried toward the door. "I'll message you later." He hated to leave, but whatever was going on was an all-hands-on-deck sort of issue, and he needed to get to the station as fast as possible.

Chase pulled into the station and parked the car before racing inside. All the other units were already responding. He got into his gear as the last of the crew arrived, and less than five minutes later, they pulled out.

"What's going on?" he asked Ed, who sat in the next rumble seat facing the rear of the truck.

"Big fire at the site of those new condos. Apparently half the places under construction are going up all at once." He shook his head.

Chase didn't want to believe the notion that raced into his head, but he was afraid the arsonist had struck again.

Piles of construction materials that had been delivered were burning, as were a number of pieces of heavy equipment. A bulldozer exploded as its gas tank ruptured. Chase joined the team of firefighters spraying foam to try to smother the searing-hot blaze.

CHAPTER 6

JERROD PUT away everything Chase had brought over. He made a trip
to Target to get the things they still needed, and he also went into the
local secondhand slash "antique" store to see what they had and came
home with an additional chair for the living room. He brought that into
the house and placed it in the room, making it less empty.

"Can we go to the park now?" Peter asked, hands on his hips like
he was at the very end of his patience.

"Let me put the last of this away and we can go in fifteen
minutes. I promise." He smiled as Peter half dragged himself up the
stairs like fifteen minutes was forever. Then he put the cutting board
and a few more kitchen things away before heading upstairs to stock
the bathroom. The list of items to get was still as long as his arm, but
he was starting to fill it in. The big thing was a mattress for his bed,
and that was on the schedule for after he took Peter to the park. "We
can go," he called to Peter, who raced out of his room just as someone
knocked on the door.

He peered out the front window before opening the door to Chase.
"Back from the fire?"

"Yeah. It was pretty bad. Those new condos they had started out off
College? A lot of the building materials and the construction equipment
just went up."

Jerrod groaned. "Great. I was supposed to start work out there in
a few weeks." What the hell was he going to do now? He had men lined
up and schedules approved and set. Now everything would be set back
by weeks or months, and it was going to be up to him to figure it all out
since he'd been the lead.

"Yeah. They were starting to get loads of basic materials, but
everything is gone."

Jerrod tried to calm the throbbing in his head. "Was it arson?"

Chase shrugged. "If I were a betting man, I'd put money on
it. The way the equipment went up, along with everything else…
someone knew what they were doing and made sure to cause as

much damage as possible." He was breathing hard, and Jerrod got him a glass of water. "Once we got there, it didn't take too long to get the fire under control, but the damage was pretty extensive. I assume that since they hadn't built too much it wasn't as bad as it could have been, but those machines are now burned-out hulks." He drank the water.

"Can we go to the park now?" Peter asked.

Jerrod didn't think it was the best timing, but he didn't want to disappoint Peter once more. "Yeah, we can go."

"Is the fireman going to come?"

"Peter, he has a name. It's Mr. Chase, remember? And I'm sure that we've taken up enough of his time today." Jerrod lifted Peter into his arms. Chase had done a lot to help them, and Jerrod didn't want to wear the man out. It was nice having Chase around, and every time he was near him, his insides did this little happy dance and he couldn't help smiling. The hardest part was that he found himself thinking about Chase when he wasn't around, wondering what he was doing and things like that. A few times over the past few days, he'd felt like a teenager again. And a lot had happened since his teenage years, that was for certain.

"I know. He's Mr. Chase, the fireman who saved me." Peter turned toward Chase. "But is he going to come with us?"

"Is that okay?" Chase asked.

Peter nodded. "You can push me on the swings."

"Oh, he can, huh?" Jerrod teased, bouncing Peter before giving him a tickle and receiving a chorus of laughter that filled the otherwise largely empty house. "Then we better go." He set Peter on his feet and got things together before trooping them off to the park.

PETER WAS worn out, which was exactly what Jerrod had hoped for after letting him run and play. He and Chase had sat at one of the picnic tables talking after Chase had indeed pushed Peter on the swings. Now that they were back home, Jerrod knew Peter wasn't going to nap, but he did quickly settle into his room for some quiet playtime.

"I can make some coffee," Jerrod offered. He didn't have anything stronger in the house.

"That would be nice." Chase sat in one of the living room chairs, and Jerrod took the other once he returned with two mismatched mugs.

"I appreciate you coming along with us. Peter has really gotten attached to you. Last night he woke up and kept asking where you were. He said you needed to save him."

"He's having bad dreams?" Chase asked.

"Yeah. I suspected he would, though I hope that over time they will dissipate. As much as I can, I try not to remind him about the fire and keep hoping that we can find a way to move on. But everything is all churned up. Staying in the hotel, moving here…."

Chase sipped from the mug and then set it on the coffee table. "Hopefully things will settle down now. I'm sure there's going to be a lot of waiting—for the insurance company, for the police, and God knows what else. But you'll keep as much of that from Peter as possible."

"I'm trying. But he asks about the way things were all the time, and he keeps wondering if this house is going to burn down too and if you're going to be around to save him." Jerrod's voice broke, and he put his mug on the table to keep his shaking hand from spilling the contents. "All I want is for him to be happy and not to have to worry about stuff like that." Sometimes he felt like such a failure. Jerrod leaned forward, his hands folded in front of him.

He almost jumped when Chase touched him, his fingers lightly gliding over Jerrod's. "None of this is your fault."

He lifted his gaze to meet Chase's. Chase's eyes filled with warmth and gentleness. "I feel like it is. If someone is coming after me… then they're coming after Peter as well, and that isn't something I can allow. He deserves to be safe and to not have to worry about his house burning down again." He sighed because there was damned little he could do about any of it. "I have smoke detectors in every room, and I lock the doors up tight whenever we leave the house. Still, I worry that when we come home…." He didn't dare finish that thought.

Chase squeezed his fingers a little more tightly. "You know all of this is probably completely normal. The worry you're both feeling seems perfectly reasonable. I think I'd be more worried if you didn't feel this way."

"You would?"

"Yeah, of course," Chase said softly. Jerrod focused his gaze on him, the way his lips parted just a little and the warmth in his eyes. Damn, he was so strong and yet kind and gentle, his touch just soft enough to comfort. Jerrod leaned forward just a little before stopping himself, but Chase drew closer. The heat between them rose quickly as Jerrod's full attention centered on Chase's touch. He closed his eyes, unable to think of anything other than the heat in that touch. Maybe it was a bad idea and he should pull away, but he couldn't bring himself to do it.

Slowly his attention widened and his gaze returned to Chase and his big, soft eyes. Without thinking, he leaned forward once more, and this time Chase did the same. Jerrod half expected an interruption—Peter from upstairs or someone knocking on the front door. But he heard nothing other than his own heart beating in his ears. The house remained quiet, and Chase drew even closer.

Jerrod exhaled softly, his lips already parting as Chase gently slipped a hand to his neck. Warmth spread through him, that touch sending a tingle all the way down his spine.

Once Chase was close enough that Jerrod felt his warm breath on his lips, he nodded slightly, and Chase closed the distance between them, kissing him gently at first before pulling back. It was so quick, Jerrod blinked a few times to make sure it had happened. But then Chase kissed him again, this time with more energy, and Jerrod returned it, deepening the kiss as he relished the warm taste of him.

"Daddy, I'm thirsty," Peter called.

Jerrod pulled back just as Peter barreled down the stairs.

Chase actually smiled. "Your son has impeccable timing."

"I want some juice," Peter said.

Jerrod got him a box from the refrigerator and helped him get the straw into it. Then Peter hurried back upstairs. "Bring the empty box back down and throw it away when you're done."

"Okay, Daddy," Peter called back down the stairs.

"That kid is a whirlwind," Chase said softly as he leaned forward. "Now, where were we?" He smiled, and Jerrod kissed him again... until the doorbell rang.

He growled and stood, went to the door, and pulled it open with more force than necessary. He stopped in his tracks at Gizelle standing outside in a yellow sundress with a bag at her feet.

"What do you want?"

"I came to see my son," she said haughtily. "I just found out what happened, and I want to make sure he's safe." She shifted a hand to her hip.

"I'm sorry, but no," Jerrod said. "Peter barely remembers you, and that's how it should be."

She narrowed her eyes, lips curling upward. "I have a right to see him. I'm his mother."

Jerrod shook his head. "Your rights were terminated years ago, before Johnny died, and that's the end of it. I know you're appealing the decision, but until you're successful with that, you have no rights here, and you need to stop acting like you do. Peter doesn't need you in his life, and it's best if you just stay away from him." Damn, he sounded harsh, but if he let her into Peter's life, what was he going to do when she disappeared again?

She actually bared her teeth at him. "You won't keep me from seeing Peter," she hissed between clenched teeth.

"I can and I will. You need to back away." Jerrod felt Chase behind him. "You have no rights here, and I don't know what you think you're doing with your bags, but…." He lowered his gaze.

"I don't have a place to go," she told him, her demeanor instantly changing.

"You aren't staying here." He shook his head. "There isn't room, and I'm not going to put up with your antics." He stepped back and closed the door, flipping the lock as Gizelle growled from outside. "God, what the hell? I'll never understand how Johnny could have gotten involved with her." He peered out the front window. Gizelle had sat down on the front step with her phone to make calls.

"Did she actually think you'd let her stay here?" Chase asked.

"God knows. With Gizelle, everything is about her. She'll demand things, then barge in. If that doesn't work, she'll try sympathy and helplessness, all within five minutes. And she thinks that people will respond to her and forget that she's a screaming lunatic. She disappears for years and then returns and expects to step right back into Peter's life." There was no way he could allow that to happen.

Chase peered out the window. "It looks like she's settling in."

"That's Gizelle—if all else fails, try to wear people down. I suspect if we ignore her, she'll find someone else to bother." Even while he said that, he had to stop himself from looking out the window too. He hated that she was there and hoped like hell that she would simply give up.

"Peter?" Chase called from the bottom of the stairs. Peter ran down the hall and then hurried to Chase. "Do you and your daddy want to come to the fire station so you can see the big trucks?"

Peter bounced like a jackrabbit. "Can I see the fire dog too?"

"We don't have one of those at the station." He turned toward Jerrod.

"Yeah. Go put your shoes on and we'll all go." Maybe it was a good idea to leave the house. Gizelle could sit on the stoop all she wanted, but she wasn't going to have an effect on an empty building. She had always thrived on drama, but she couldn't cause any if they ignored her. It was the one thing Gizelle hated more than anything.

"Okay." Peter hurried back upstairs and returned with his shoes on. He bounced through the house as Jerrod made sure the front door was locked. Then he pulled open the back, holding Peter's hand as he locked the door behind him and then headed down the street to Jerrod's truck. He got Peter buckled in the back seat and then climbed in with Chase as passenger, leaving Gizelle behind without a single word to her. Maybe now she'd get the idea that she didn't have a place here, and if she wanted something, she needed to ask, rather than try to demand it.

Jerrod drove to the station while Chase made a call ahead. As they pulled in, the overhead doors were up, and Peter got out, looking at the trucks with his mouth open. "They're huge."

"They have to be because they have to have all the stuff we need," Chase said before showing Peter the big hook-and-ladder truck. "We can extend that until it's really high. And that one has a big tank so we can bring water to a fire when there isn't some around."

"You could use a hose," Peter said. "Daddy has those."

"You could," Chase said, "but see how much bigger these are than the hoses at home? That means we can put more water on the fire and put it out faster."

Jerrod stood back as Chase explained what each truck and piece of equipment was used for. He also showed Peter their gear and how they used it.

"That's what you were wearing when you saved me?" Peter said at Chase's fire suit. He touched the pants with a sense of awe.

"That's what all firefighters do. We always try to keep everybody safe. That's what all this equipment is for. We have ladders so we can put the fire out and get to anyone who might be trapped inside, like you were."

Peter looked up at Chase, his eyes shining with hero worship. "Will you always be there if I need help?"

Chase grinned. "I'll try. That I can promise you." One of the other firefighters wandered out to join them. "This is Hayden. He and I work together."

"Are you a hero like Mr. Chase?" Peter asked.

"Being a hero isn't our job. It's just helping people," Hayden said. "That's what we do." He stood next to Chase. Jerrod remembered Hayden from the initial meeting he'd had about the fire report. There didn't seem to be any bad feelings, which he was relieved about. Hayden let Peter try on his fire hat, and Jerrod took pictures.

"We should go in case they have to help someone," Jerrod told Peter. "Give the hat back to Mr. Hayden and we can go home." Hopefully Gizelle would be gone by the time they returned.

"But I wanna ride in the truck," Peter said, pointing to the cab.

"Sorry, buddy, but that I can't do for you. There are lots of rules about rides." Chase smiled and handed Hayden back his hat. "Thank you for helping," he told him. He stayed behind to talk a minute while Jerrod got Peter buckled in the back of the truck.

"Was that fun?" Jerrod asked as they waited for Chase.

"Yes. The ladder is so big," Peter said, smiling.

"Mr. Chase was very nice to bring you here."

"Yes, Daddy." Peter laughed and then grew quiet for a few seconds. "I saw you and him kissing." He giggled some more. "Boys are supposed to kiss girls."

Jerrod sighed. He had hoped to put off this talk, but then again, they probably should have been more careful. "Boys can kiss boys too. It's perfectly okay. You kiss people who are special to you." He hoped that settled the issue, at least for now.

Jerrod was still trying to figure this out when Chase climbed into the truck. "Daddy and Chasey sitting in a tree, k-i-s-s-i-n-g," Peter sang.

Jerrod rolled his eyes.

"I see." Chase turned and grinned at Peter before tickling him, earning a peal of high-pitched laughter. Peter settled when Chase turned back around, and at the drive, Jerrod made a left toward town. The tension in the cab grew the closer he got to the house.

The stoop was empty as Jerrod pulled to a stop in front of the house. There didn't seem to be any sign of Gizelle. He got out and helped Peter down, then unlocked the door and went inside.

He nearly lost his shit when Gizelle stood up from one of his chairs.

"What are you doing in here?" Jerrod demanded, holding on to his temper by a thread.

"Someone from down the street approached me, and I told them I was waiting for you. He was nice enough to let me in." She actually smiled like she had put one over on him. "I wasn't sure where to put my things…."

"Chase, please take Peter upstairs," Jerrod said, grinding his teeth he was so angry. Chase followed Jerrod's instructions, and Peter followed him up the stairs. Then Jerrod turned on his former sister-in-law. "Get out now," he told her, his voice as menacing as he could make it. "As far as I'm concerned, you're a trespasser, and I have the right to protect my home." He drew closer and pulled himself as upright as possible. "You get out right the hell now. You are not welcome here." He picked up her bags, went to the door, and tossed them onto the sidewalk.

"But—" she began.

"Out. Never come back here again, and this incident will be reported to the court. Your parental rights were terminated, gone, done, over. You need help, and you need to get it. But you're not going to stay here."

"My son…." Her words were almost plaintive.

"You should have thought about that before walking out on your family and disappearing completely. Peter doesn't even remember you, and I'm not going to have you hurt him again." He pointed to the door. "Now, you get out and stay away or I will throw you out, and I'm mad enough to toss your backside all the way across the street." It was only a threat. In truth, his mother had deeply ingrained in him to not hit other people, but Gizelle didn't know that, and finally she headed for the door. As soon as she stepped outside, he closed and locked it behind her.

Jerrod stood in the middle of the living room, heaving in deep breaths as he tried to calm down. "Are you okay?" Chase asked as he came downstairs. Jerrod turned toward him, and Chase engulfed him in a hug. Almost instantly, the tension that had threatened to burst him into a million pieces backed away and leached out of him.

"What am I going to do?" Jerrod whispered as he held Chase tightly, wondering what he had ever done to deserve this.

CHAPTER 7

CHASE LOVED having Jerrod in his arms. Not the circumstances, but holding him like this was amazing. He didn't say anything right away, just let the quiet settle around them, hoping it would help Jerrod.

"I just don't know what else could go wrong," Jerrod whispered, making no move to step away.

"I think you need to contact the landlord and let them know what happened. They should never have let anyone inside the house under any circumstances." Hell, what they had done was illegal, but Chase wasn't sure pointing that out would be beneficial. "Then we can inform the court that terminated her rights that she is causing trouble and try to get a restraining order. That will help keep her away from you."

"I don't know. Gizelle will still be Gizelle," Jerrod said.

Chase stepped back slightly, his hands on Jerrod's shoulders. "That's true. But then the police will be able to help you easily. If there's a restraining order, then there's also a presumption of guilt on her part, and the police will take her away and the court will decide her punishment for violating the order."

Jerrod shrugged. "I can't afford all that. What money I have is going to making sure I can give Peter a home. Everything is just getting to be so much." He sighed softly and pulled away. "I feel like the walls are closing in, and I have no idea how much closer they're going to get." He wiped his eyes. "I promised Johnny that I'd watch out for Peter if anything happened to him. I never thought when I agreed that I'd have to. Johnny was young and strong. But look what's come of it. Peter was nearly killed in a fire because someone wanted to get even with me for some slight. And now his crazy mother has decided to come back. I don't know if Peter is still in danger, and…."

The world seemed to be settling on Jerrod's shoulders, and Chase knew there was nothing he could do about it. When Jerrod turned again, Chase tugged him back into his arms. This time he kissed him hard just because Jerrod needed to know that he was there. This wasn't a kiss of passion as much as care and comfort, but with Jerrod, it only took a few seconds for the feeling to shift. But Chase had to hold back.

This was not the time to get carried away, though just being near Jerrod made his blood race. It was the rich scent of him, the gentleness in his eyes, and even the way he doubted himself when Chase could see how strong he really was. Chase pulled back, if only to stop himself from taking things further.

"What do I do to keep Peter safe? That's all I care about," Jerrod asked.

"We stay vigilant," Chase told him. "Do you think Gizelle could have been behind the fire?"

Jerrod shook his head. "I doubt it. I don't think she can plan that methodically. Everything with her is about how she feels and what she wants in the moment." He paused for a few seconds and then shrugged. "God, I have no idea. Maybe she thought that making us homeless would somehow give her an advantage. I don't know. I suppose she could have. My head is spinning, and I don't know what to think anymore. I do know that the only way we are going to figure out who is behind this is to try to gather some evidence in order to pick this mystery apart. We certainly aren't going to get anywhere trying to think it out."

"We aren't." But this wasn't something Chase had done before. The police should handle it, but they hadn't even contacted Jerrod yet about the arson at his home, so they weren't likely to get to the bottom of it. "I need to speak with Hayden and see if he can help us."

"Isn't he the guy who thought that my work had started the fire? The guy who was with us today?" Jerrod seemed edgy.

"It is. But he updated his report, and he doesn't seem like he's holding a grudge. I bet he wants to get to the bottom of this as much as we do."

"So you really think he'll help?"

Chase nodded. "I thought we might ask him to come for a beer. We can see what he thinks and if he's found out anything about the fire earlier today." He really believed the fires were linked, but he wasn't sure how. Chase felt it was premature to say that Jerrod was the reason, but that seemed to the best guess they had.

"Okay."

"Also…." Chase's mind ran a mile a minute. "Can you give me the full names of the two men you let go? I want to see if I can speak to them. Maybe feel them out a little to see if they might know something."

Jerrod nodded. "I had to look them up for the police. It's Steve Wilson and Gary Lutz. I don't think there's anything secret about them working for me. The union would have records of it."

"True. You can't release any personal information you might have, but their names should be okay." He was already trying to think of how he could track them down, but Chase had always been resourceful. Social media was often a great method for finding out basic pieces of information.

"Okay." He went to the kitchen and wrote down the names, then returned with a sheet of paper that he handed Chase. "A lot of my job history records might have gone up in the fire. I kept most of my files in the house."

"Where were they kept?" Chase asked.

"I had file drawers in my office, which was upstairs next to Peter's room. I don't know if that part of the house survived."

Chase nodded slowly. "Let me see if it's possible to check on them and how safe that section of the house is." He hummed softly to himself. "Maybe there's something in your records that someone didn't want anyone to see."

Jerrod shrugged. "It's possible, but what? That's my receipts and records for tax purposes. What could someone want with that? There are employee files and that sort of thing, but I don't know how that could be a threat to anyone." He sat down, and Chase did the same in the other chair.

"I suppose we aren't going to know until we can take a look."

"True," Jerrod said. "But I can't ask you to do all that." He shook his head slowly. "I feel helpless."

"All I'm going to do is get permission to go up the back stairs and check on the state of the office. As for Hayden, it's just a quick conversation to see if he'll help us." Chase leaned across the space between them. "Let me go and see what I can find out, and I'll let you know as soon as I can."

"Okay."

Chase got to his feet and kissed Jerrod gently before leaving. He needed to get to the station before it got too late to talk to anyone.

"WHY DO you need to go inside again?" the captain asked as he leaned back at his desk. "You were just in the house yesterday."

"Then can the owner go inside? There are some business records that he needs. We don't know if they survived the fire, and the owner needs to know if he'll have to recreate them somehow." That was as good an explanation as he could think of without raising too many additional questions.

"I got a note that the building has been condemned as unsafe for habitation by the borough, so it all has to come down. The police have been inside, but I don't know what they did or found. So as far as I know, he might be able to go there as long as he's careful."

"I thought I'd go with him. If it's too dangerous, then he'll have to find another way to get what he needs. Thanks, Captain. I appreciate the help." Chase left him to get back to work and smiled to himself. At least he'd managed part one of what he needed to do. He strode through to the break room, where Hayden sat at the table, drinking his coffee.

"What's up?"

"Do you have a minute?" Chase asked, and Hayden stood and followed him out into the hall. "Did you find anything at the fire today?" Hayden nodded, his eyes narrowing suspiciously. "Can you tell me what you found?"

Hayden paused. "Let's just say that I was surprised to find a couple melted electrical caps and the remains of some wire and metal. It was very familiar."

Chase leaned against the wall. "So you think it was the same person?"

"I can't discuss that right now. The police are working on what we uncovered, and it would be bad form to step on their toes." Hayden's gaze was as serious as a heart attack. "There were a lot of similarities to what we've found before. Why?"

"Because if that's true, it may be connected. Jerrod told me that he was expecting to start work at that site in a few weeks." He let the implications settle with Hayden.

"So you think that the fire may have been set because someone is trying to hurt Jerrod? At a job site he hadn't started working at yet? That seems a little farfetched, but there's a definite link." Hayden didn't seem to know what to think. "It could be that we have a firebug and that the only real link between the fires is the person who set them."

Chase had to admit that was possible. "I know. But we can't ignore any possible leads, which is why I brought you the information."

Hayden put his hands up. "Okay. You're right. I can meet with you guys to talk tomorrow after our shift. Maybe he has something that can help with all this. I've been in touch with Red at the borough police department, and he said that he was looking into this."

"Invite him to join us if he wants. Maybe if we all put our heads together, something will stand out." Maybe Chase was too new and naïve, but it certainly couldn't hurt.

"All right. I'll make a call and let you know tomorrow."

"Thanks." Chase left the station and headed to Jerrod's house.

CHASE STOOD outside the burned-out shell, the upper front windows like square black eyes devoid of life. Where that came from he had no idea. With a scoff at his own whimsy, Chase walked around to the back. He carefully went inside, the scent of burned wood stinging his nose. Going up the stairs, he was cautious, testing the floor the way he had the last time he'd been here. Chase checked what had been Peter's room, more out of habit than anything else. Then he moved to the next door closer to the front of the house and pushed it open.

The wall closest to the front was mostly intact. It smelled heavily of smoke. The plaster was wet, with part of the ceiling hanging down. The desk sat near the partially burned wall, the papers soggy and sticking to the top. A single file cabinet sat just inside the door. Chase tested the floor and approached the cabinet, then pulled it toward the door and out into the hall, where he knew the footing was safer.

The three top drawers held files, and he pulled each one out and carried it down to the truck. The bottom drawer held supplies and various things Jerrod might have stashed there. He took that drawer as well before peering into the room once more. He wasn't sure if he should try to check in the desk, but halfway across the room, he felt the floor begin to give, so he backed away and out of the room again, then closed the door behind him. He left the house just as a crash sounded from inside, followed by a bang and splintering wood. "Shit," he groaned under his breath before peering in the side window. The floor had given way, and what was left of the desk lay in pieces on the floor below. He'd gotten what he could, and it was pretty clear that nothing more could be safely removed from the house.

He drove to Jerrod's rental house. Jerrod met him at the front door. "Did you get the files?"

"Yeah. I had to leave the cabinet, but I took the drawers." He blinked and sighed.

"What happened?"

"After I got the files, I tried to see if I could get to the desk." He shook his head. "I must have destabilized the floor, because it came down after I left the building."

Jerrod nodded. "At least you weren't hurt. That's all that matters." He got him inside and hugged him tight. "I can replace the desk and everything else." He stepped back. "You shouldn't have gone in there alone. What if something had happened?"

"I'm fine. Let's get these file drawers inside. The clouds are building. The file cabinet seems to have kept the papers dry, so we don't want them soaked now by a rainstorm."

They carried the drawers inside and placed them in the corner of the small dining area. "Hayden said he could come over tomorrow after our shift, and he was going to see if one of the guys from the police could come too." Chase sat down in what was starting to feel like his usual chair. "I don't know if he's convinced that the two arson cases are related, but he did hint that they found the same types of debris at your home as at the construction site."

"But that proves it," Jerrod said.

"It only proves that it could be the same person, not that you're the reason for both of them. This could be a firebug situation. And he's right. It's possible." Chase sat back. "But I don't believe it. I think we have to go with the assumption that this is about you, if only because we can stay vigilant in order to keep you and Peter safe." Dismissing their possible involvement was a way to let their guard down, and Chase had no intention of allowing that to happen.

"So what do we do?"

"Look through your files to see if we can find the information on anyone you let go, someone who might hold a grudge. We can give it to the police, and we'll look for any sort of pattern. I'm not sure if there is anything to find, but we need to look." Chase had no idea what they might be checking for, but he was willing to help.

"It's okay. Mostly there are tax records and receipts for various jobs and supplies. One of the drawers held the details of people I worked with, but most of them were contractors like me. They had their own businesses and weren't employees of mine, so there isn't going to be any detailed personal information."

"Okay. Well, let's go take a look and see if there is anything at all." Chase stood, and Jerrod did the same.

"I think I'm going to put on a pot of coffee. We'll need it."

CHAPTER 8

JERROD SET aside the last of his tax records and leaned back, stretching his arms. Chase sat in the chair across from him, the coffee table strewn with papers and items of interest.

"What do you have?" Jerrod asked.

Chase set down another partially crumpled pink invoice. "I'm not sure." He picked up the pile and handed it to him. "These are all payment slips from West Electric, and they're fairly consistent. But then three months ago, they took a jump." He leaned closer, his sweat and musk making it difficult for Jerrod to think.

"I have an account set up. It's paid automatically, and they send me the invoices, which I file." He sighed, feeling kind of stupid. "I probably should have looked more closely, but with work and Peter, I don't have a lot of time."

"Okay. Just take a look at them now." He flipped through and tapped the point that they changed. "You were spending about a thousand a month, and suddenly it's three or so." He pointed again, and Jerrod returned to the other files to grab the detailed invoices. "I didn't order this stuff." He set the detailed listing on the table and went through it, marking things. "This isn't right." His hand shook as he continued going through all the items.

Once he'd gone through one month, he went through the others and found the same sort of items on the subsequent reports. It looked as though he was either being cheated by West or someone was putting stuff on his account. "There's, like, six thousand dollars here. No wonder I've been working like a dog and scraping the bottom of the barrel each month."

"This would explain it. Not that it gets us any closer to who might want to hurt you."

Jerrod put the pages aside. "I'm not so sure. How far is it from theft to arson? Someone was willing to steal from me for months…." He was so angry he could barely see straight. West Electric was closed at the moment, but he knew the number of the agent he always worked with.

"What are you doing?"

His hand shook as he found the number in his contacts. "Kurt," he said when the call answered.

"Hey, Jerrod. How is it going? I'm so sorry to hear about the house. Are you and Peter okay? What do you need? I talked to the boss, and he said to make sure you had everything you needed to get you through the next few months."

"Well, I'm calling about the last few months. There are a number of items on my invoice that I didn't order. Thousands of dollars' worth. I know you aren't always there, but maybe you could ask around to figure out what's happening."

"I check your invoice every month before it's sent for payment. Everything on there was added by you or one of your guys. They should have given you the order slips."

Jerrod paused. "Kurt, I don't have any guys who come in for me."

Kurt was silent. "Steve Wilson came in a few months ago and said he was working for you now and needed some things."

Jerrod thought he was going to be sick. "I fired his ass after a week. The guy did shoddy work. I never sent him in for supplies. I never trusted him enough." Holy shit. "I thought I...." He stood and started pacing. "Goddammit."

"Hold on a minute," Kurt said. "I can log in to work from home." He set the phone aside, and Jerrod heard him typing. "Yes, I always make a note of who picks up the orders." He typed for a while. "I can see all of the ones he placed." He groaned. "This is as much our fault as anything. We should have checked. He told us he was working for you in April."

"I canned him at the end of March. I can give you a copy of the paperwork to prove it."

"Then give me a minute." Kurt worked, and Jerrod brought Chase up to date.

"He was stealing from me. Putting stuff on my account."

"Steve was in today and placed an order. I changed the account to his on that one and the others that haven't been paid yet." Kurt continued working while Jerrod fumed. Chase placed a hand on Jerrod's shoulder. "Okay, I have them all. They have Steve's name on them but were charged to you. I'm going to call Rosemary to let her know what happened and find out how she wants to handle this. Let me call you back." Kurt hung up.

Jerrod wanted to throw the phone against the wall, he was so frustrated. And as busy as he was, he might not have noticed the issue for months—until he was completely broke—if Chase hadn't spotted it.

"I take it you know him—Kurt," Chase said.

"There have been times when a client needed some help right away and I didn't have something I needed. He always came in to help. Kurt is a really good guy, and the guy using my account was Steve Wilson—one of the two men I fired." He smiled as his phone rang.

"Jerrod, it's Kurt again. Rosemary said to transfer all the purchases to Steve's account and to issue you a refund to the card we have on file. She said she wants to see Steve the next time he comes in, and he can either make the account right or she'll report him for theft." One thing was for sure, you did not want to get on the bad side of Rosemary West. She was hell on wheels, and if she dropped Steve as a customer for something like this, she would make sure everyone knew why.

"Thanks, Kurt, and tell Rosemary that I appreciate her support and help as well."

"No problem at all." Kurt hung up, and Jerrod flopped back down in his chair just as Peter came downstairs and climbed into his lap, like he knew Jerrod needed a hug. Jerrod put his arms around his son and leaned back in his chair, taking comfort from his unusually quiet son.

"Are you okay, Daddy?" Peter asked.

"I am now," he answered softly, holding Peter. Hearing Peter call him Daddy never got old. He had always called Johnny Papa, but it was about three months after Johnny's death before Peter started calling him that.

"I'm going to wish both of you a good night, and I'll see you after my shift tomorrow." Chase gave him a smile and took his hand, squeezing it a few times before letting go. Then he left, closing the door behind him.

Peter rested his head against Jerrod's chest, and Jerrod closed his eyes, trying to hold the tension and anxiety that always seemed to show up whenever he was alone at bay. For now, holding Peter kept him calm, but he knew that wouldn't last.

"Come on. Let's get you a snack before going to bed," Jerrod whispered, and Peter slipped off his lap. Jerrod got Peter a plate of cheese and crackers, which he ate at the coffee table. Then they went upstairs, and Jerrod helped Peter get ready for bed and tucked him in.

After reading Peter a story, he went back downstairs and sat in one of the chairs. If he had a television, he might have turned it on to try to find something mind-numbing. But instead he grabbed a light blanket and leaned back, pulling it up over him. What he really needed to do was get a mattress and have it delivered so he could have a proper bed, but it wasn't like he was going to be able to sleep anyway. He hadn't since the fire. Every time he closed his eyes, he began to worry about what would happen if the person who set the fire returned. So for the past week, he'd slept in fits and starts. With a sigh, he settled in, turning off the lights, hoping he might get some rest, but knowing it was going to be a long night.

"Is Mr. Chase coming?" Peter asked the following afternoon, peering out the front window. "He said he would be here." He turned away and hurried out of the room and back up the stairs, then came down with a crayon picture that he put on the coffee table.

"Did you make that for him?" Jerrod asked from his chair. It felt like he hadn't moved since last night, but somehow he'd made it through his workday. Now he hoped he'd get a chance to rest. The truth was that he was exhausted and seemed to be getting more so all the time.

"Yes." He brought it over to show Jerrod, but sounds outside drew him back to the window. "He's here." Peter rushed to the door and pulled it open before Jerrod could get up.

"Hey, buddy," Chase said in his rich voice.

"I made this for you." Peter was in top energetic form, which made Jerrod feel even more lethargic. Peter handed Chase the drawing, and he ooohed and aahed over it, to Peter's delight.

"I'm going to put this where I can see it every day," Chase told him.

Peter ran upstairs, probably to make more pictures, while Chase greeted Jerrod with a dark look and a gentle kiss that Jerrod felt to his toes.

A knock made Jerrod jump slightly. Chase answered the door. "I take it this is the right place. I'm Red with the borough police. Hayden asked me to stop by. But if I'm interrupting something…. Terry is always telling me that I have the worst timing."

Jerrod stood and greeted Red with a handshake. "I think we've met, but I can't remember where."

"The bookstore downtown," Red said.

Jerrod nodded. "That's it. You were doing one of their reading programs. It's good to see you again, and I really appreciate your help with whatever is going on."

Red nodded as another knock sounded, and Chase let Hayden inside. Then Red took charge. "What do you have?" he asked.

Jerrod led them to the kitchen table with the mismatched chairs he'd found at a charity store in town. "Okay. If I'm speaking out of turn, let me know. But so far there have been two fires that seem similar. One took Peter's and my home, and another burned the building site north of town. I was supposed to start work there in a few weeks. Not that I'm trying to be narcissistic, but that's a possible connection."

"We're looking into that," Hayden said.

"Chase and I went through records he was able to get from the house, and we found that one of the men I fired a few months ago has been putting supplies on my account at West Electric. I don't know if he bid on the job at the complex that burned, but it's likely." Everything seemed to be spilling out all at once.

"Okay. Let's take this one step at a time," Red said before having Jerrod and Chase walk him through the issue with Steve. "And you can prove that he tried to steal from you?"

"Kurt at West Electric can back me up. They have the detailed records, and he said that Steve told him he was working for me after I let him go." God, this was starting to sound like the plot from a bad movie. "They are handling the issue, and either Steve will pay what he owes or they will get the police involved. But…."

"Let me guess. You made a list of suspects, and he was on it," Red said.

"We tried to figure out who might have a grudge against Jerrod and who might want to hurt him. Someone set fire to his home and did the same at the construction site." Chase stood next to Hayden, his gaze hard. "We thought you might want to know all the information we have."

"I do. Don't get me wrong," Red explained. "Who else was on your list of suspects?"

"A second person I had to let go—Gary Lutz. He was worse than Steve. And then my ex-sister-in-law, Gizelle. She's Peter's mother, but her rights were terminated because she abandoned Peter years ago. Now she's back in town and has been causing trouble."

"Are those the only people on your list?" Red asked.

Jerrod looked at Chase and shrugged. "It isn't like I go around trying to make enemies. I'm an electrician, and I'm trying to make a living so I can support myself and Peter. I don't have grand plans about trying to take on the world or shake up the electrical contracting industry. I usually do residential work, but lately I've been bidding on some of the larger projects, and some of those have been accepted."

Red leaned closer. "Who have been the other bidders? Do you know?"

"I don't," Jerrod said, but Red wrote something down anyway.

"Give me a list of the bids that you've won and who the general contractor is. I have some contacts, and I can do some digging to see whose side you might have become a thorn in. Maybe someone decided to hit back."

Jerrod thought for a few minutes and provided Red with the information. It wasn't like he bid on a ton of jobs, so the list wasn't huge. "The biggest one was the condo complex they're building. That was the largest job I ever tried to go for, and I've got good people lined up to work with me. But now with the fire, who knows what's going to happen? Then there's the fire at my house. The insurance company is dragging its feet because I haven't been ruled out as a suspect. So I'm stuck with my business threatened, and I lost my home." His hand shook, and Chase took it.

"That's part of why everyone is here. We have to try to get things on track."

"You have never been an arson suspect. You weren't home when the fire started, but your son was. And there is no indication that you benefited from the fire in any way." Red made more notes. "Let me go through the files so I can make a few things clear, and then I'll let you know that the updates have been made so you can contact the insurance company again. That should free up some resources for you." He continued making notes. "I'm also going to speak to the captain to see if I can have this case transferred to me. Then maybe I can take a closer look and get to the bottom of it."

"Thank you." Jerrod didn't know what else to say as the conversation swirled around him.

Hayden gave an account what they found at both locations, and Chase listened, but didn't seem to have too much to add. It seemed that both locations had the same type of debris, which led to the conclusion that it was the same person behind both fires.

"Has there been a fire like this in the past?" Jerrod asked. Everyone turned toward him. "Maybe there's something in the records to shed light on this. What if these aren't the first fires set this way, just the first ones we know about?" That seemed to stop everyone in their tracks.

"That's a great idea," Hayden said. "I can try to search through the department records and see what I come up with."

"I can help," Chase offered. "One of the captains might remember something as well."

"I can check at the department too, but arson investigations usually start with the fire department, so you might have more information than we do." Red made a few more notes and closed his book. "Is there anything else you can think of?"

"Not really," Jerrod said. "But if I think of anything, I'll be sure to let everyone know." He stood, and the others did the same. Then Red and Hayden left the house.

"Are they all going?" Peter asked as Jerrod lifted him into his arms.

"Where have you been?"

"Making pictures," Peter answered and smiled.

"Are they upstairs?" He set Peter down. "I'd like to see them, okay?"

Peter hurried upstairs and came down with a stack of drawings. "This is you." He flipped the page. "And this one is Mr. Chase." He showed them yet another drawing. "This is a dinosaur. Rrrrrrr."

"They're really good," Chase told him. "Maybe you'll be an artist when you grow up."

Peter shook his head. "Nope. Gonna be a fireman so I can save kids like you did." He smiled and then put the drawings on the coffee table.

"What do you want for dinner?"

"Cheesy pasta," Peter said. "The box kind."

Jerrod made a face. Peter loved the stuff, but the thought made Jerrod's stomach rebel. There was nothing worse as far as he was concerned. "Okay. I'll make you some."

"I should probably go. I know you and Peter have things you need to do...."

"Well, I can make us something more grown-up if you can wait a little while. I need to get Peter fed and in bed, but then I have something I can make for us." Jerrod went into the kitchen to get things together, while Chase followed. He pulled out a bottle of wine and a couple glasses, then poured one for each of them.

"This is pretty good."

"I got it at the state store. It isn't too bad. They had it on sale, so I picked up a couple bottles. They must have overbought." He took a sip and put water on to boil as Chase leaned against the doorway just inside Jerrod's line of sight, sipping from his glass. Jerrod nearly forgot to remove the cheese packet from the box before dumping the macaroni in the water. Chase slowly drew closer as he stirred the pot, trying to pay attention to the water rather than the real heat washing off Chase.

"You know you need to let me finish this." He swallowed hard as Chase moved him away from the stove before pressing him against the counter next to the sink. "Chase...."

"Do you have any idea how hot you are?" His voice was rough.

Jerrod rolled his eyes. "What I am is a mess. I can't seem to get anything together or figure out what the hell is going on. It feels like my life is falling apart, and yet...." He found it difficult to continue talking. "God, I just want to make it all go away."

Chase nestled closer. "I know how we can do that."

"Yeah, I bet you do. But there's just one problem... well, more than one. Peter is just upstairs, and as much as I would love you to help me forget everything for just a little while, he definitely needs to be in bed. And speaking of beds, I don't have one yet."

Chase paused his lips right behind Jerrod's ear, little tingles of desire washing through him with every gentle touch. Jerrod closed his eyes, whimpering and wishing he could hold the sound inside. Every cell in his body cried out for Chase, wishing he could hold him the whole night long. He wanted to know what it felt like to have that intense, hard body pressed to him and feel the energy that Chase exuded wash over him. But practicality combined with footsteps on the stairs forced them apart and poured the cold water of reality over them both.

Jerrod had so much upheaval in his life right now, and as he returned his attention to Peter's dinner, he couldn't help wondering if this was the best timing for what seemed to be happening between him and Chase. What if this was just an infatuation brought on by the fact that he felt so untethered at the moment? Chase was strong and a real leader. Maybe Jerrod was simply latching on to him because those characteristics were what he needed right now. And he couldn't help wondering if this was the time to start a relationship. He shook his head slightly, pulling himself out of his musings as he stirred the pasta to give himself something to do.

"Is it almost ready?" Peter asked. "I'm hungry."

"Me too," Chase said, meeting Jerrod's gaze with enough fire in his eyes for Jerrod to spill water over the top of the stove.

"Okay. This needs just a couple more minutes." He got a bowl out of the cupboard and set it on the counter, giving himself a chance to catch his breath. Then, purposely not looking at Chase, he drained the pasta and added some butter and milk before stirring in the cheese powder.

"Thank you, Daddy," Peter said when Jerrod handed him his bowl.

"You're welcome," he told Peter, who hurried to the secondhand table in the corner of the kitchen to eat.

"How about I order us something for dinner? You seem worn out, and there's no need to cook for me," Chase offered.

"It's okay. I'm not really hungry anyway. I can make you something, though."

"That isn't necessary. I'll go and let you and Peter get some rest."

Fatigue bloomed in him, and Jerrod nodded. "Thanks. I'll see you later." He led Chase to the door and kissed him goodbye before closing and locking it behind him. He hated to see Chase go, and yet maybe without him here, he would have a chance to think.

He ate a few bites of Peter's mac and cheese, which did nothing to stoke his appetite. Then he got Peter into bed before settling in his chair, hoping he might get a little sleep and wishing he could stop the roller coaster of fear and anxiety he spent nearly every night riding.

CHAPTER 9

"Did you find anything?" Chase asked Hayden the following afternoon.

"Maybe," Hayden answered. "It's hard to tell because the report isn't written up the exact same way." He angled the computer screen so Chase could see it. "Look at this report from six months ago. The fire was ruled accidental, but look at what was found near the starting point." Hayden pointed to the words.

"Melted bits of plastic," Chase said. "Though they don't identify what they were, you think it could be the same sort of thing that we found."

"Yeah."

"Then why didn't we find it earlier? The department isn't that big." Chase's mind raced forward.

"This is a report from Mount Holly. The fire happened down there. I didn't find anything in our files, so I made a few calls and got access to a few other departments' online material, where I found this."

"That's cool, though I don't know what it tells us, other than that Jerrod's fire isn't the first." He drummed his fingers on the top of Hayden's desk. "We need to tell Red. Maybe he's come up with something." It wasn't as though they could track the various people they had as possible suspects.

"What I need you to do is talk to Jerrod and see if he has any link to this property or anyone who might have lived there. Maybe that can help us narrow things down. This could be just a coincidence." Hayden went back to his work, and Chase wondered if they had just stumbled onto something bigger than what he or Hayden had thought possible.

"I will." He wandered back down to the trucks to get back to work. A rural call first thing that morning had left the trucks covered in mud, which meant they needed to be washed from top to bottom, so they were being pulled out of the station one by one, and he needed to help.

"Not quite what you thought being a firefighter would be?" Larry, a firefighter who had been there for a year or so, asked.

"We have to keep the equipment clean and ready," Chase told him, but Larry just rolled his eyes before dropping his sponge back in his bucket.

"If I wanted to work at a car wash, I could have worked for my father," he sighed. Chase had heard that Larry's father owned the old car wash on South Hanover, one of those that you could drive into and wash your car yourself for a couple bucks.

"Knock it off and finish up. There's still another truck to do." Chase didn't get a chance to see who said it as he grabbed a sponge and got to work. There was plenty to do before the next call came in, which happened only five minutes later, and they all jumped into their gear and headed out, the truck still dripping water behind them.

THEIR CALL, which wasn't a fire, involved them deploying their ladder to get a kid out of a tree on Louther. He'd climbed too high and couldn't get down. Back at the station, Chase went inside to get something to drink before pitching in to finish the cleanup.

"Chase," Hayden called just as he finished polishing the valves on the side of the pumper.

"Yeah." He set his supplies aside and jogged to where Hayden stood near the overhead door. "What's up?"

"I found two more," he said, and Chase felt himself pale. "I think this is a lot bigger than we thought."

"Okay." Chase followed Hayden inside. "So do you think it's a firebug?"

Hayden shook his head as he drew a chair to his desk for Chase. "No. It's not that simple. These fires were purposeful. Firebugs don't generally have a hidden agenda. They set fires because they like to watch things burn. There's a magic in the flames for them. They get a thrill out of it and often meld into the crowd so they can watch their handiwork." He typed for a while. "I don't see that happening here."

"Okay." Chase wasn't sure what Hayden was getting at, but he didn't think he was going to like it.

"The fire in Mount Holly, the one I showed you earlier, was at a small restaurant. The place went up fast because of the supplies that were stored there. The fire was ruled an accident. I turned the info over to Red, and he called me back while you were out on a call. He said that the owner received harassing calls demanding money starting a few weeks before the fire. They apparently refused to pay...."

"Oh God." Chase turned to Hayden. "Do we really have that sort of thing in this area?" It seemed unfathomable.

"Highway 81 runs right around town and then up into New York from the south. It's a major artery for illicit activity, and unfortunately, it looks like someone has decided to set up shop here and didn't like that the restaurant owners weren't playing ball."

"So you think the same thing happened to Jerrod? I'm sure he would have told us."

Hayden shrugged. "I don't know. But it's one more thing to ask about." He turned back to the computer screen. "The more I dig into what started as a house fire, the more dirt I uncover, and it's frightening."

Chase had to agree with him. "Maybe we need to turn all this over to the police. We did our fire investigation. Now they need to do theirs and get to the bottom of the criminal angle." His phone vibrated in his pocket, and Chase tensed when he saw Jerrod's name.

"Hey, what's up?" Chase asked.

"I'm on a job, and the homeowner is here. She's an elderly lady who has difficulty getting around, and I'm putting in the power so she can install a chair lift. She says there are people outside the house that shouldn't be there, and it's got her a little upset." He lowered his voice, and Chase strained to hear him. "They keep pointing at the house and.... I know I'm a little spooked, but I don't know what to do. Maybe I'm overreacting." He grew quiet. "What? They're what?" he asked. "Mrs. Gunderson says that it looks like they're messing with my truck."

"Call the police. Right now. If you have a fob, make the alarm go off. See if you can scare them. Make sure you get a good look at them in case anything is wrong. Call me as soon as you know anything."

"Okay." Jerrod hung up.

Chase told Hayden what Jerrod had told him. "I hope it's not what it sounds like."

"I know. Not that I blame him at all." Hayden went back to his computer, and Chase stood and went back to cleaning the equipment and hoping that everything was okay.

"WHAT HAPPENED?" Chase asked as soon as Jerrod answered the phone. He'd been waiting an hour and had done his best to try to keep his mind focused on his work.

"The police just left. One of the tires on my truck had been slashed. Mrs. G gave the police a real good description of the guys, and they are looking for them now." He sounded more in control than he had when he called the first time. "I was able to finish the work and got the spare on the truck. So now I just have to get a new spare and I'll be okay."

"Did you find out what they wanted in the first place?"

"Not really. I'm hoping that the police can find them and get to the bottom of this," Jerrod said. "But they're gone now, and Mrs. G is happy. She took my side and gave the police a lot of information. She may have trouble getting around, but that lady is as sharp as a tack."

"Good. I'm glad you're okay." Chase wondered if he should tell Jerrod what they'd found and suspected, but he held off. There was still a lot of the picture that had yet to come into focus, and that wasn't the kind of information that you told people over the phone. "I'll talk to you when I'm through with my shift." One of his team was calling him, so he hung up and joined them back at the truck to finish up the cleaning.

By the end of his shift, they'd had two more calls, and Chase was exhausted. Hayden didn't know much more than he had before, but he said he'd contacted Red and sent him everything he'd found. "I wish I could say he was surprised, but Red seemed to take it in stride. He said he was going to get in contact with your friend Jerrod." Hayden continued out of the station and out to his truck. "I'll see you tomorrow."

Chase nodded and stood out front, looking across the street, his thoughts growing deeper. In some ways, it felt strange that Hayden had uncovered what he had and yet seemed unfazed by it. It was probably inexperience on Chase's part and the fact that everything was new. Or maybe Hayden had simply learned to compartmentalize things enough that he was able to leave his job at work.

Except this wasn't Chase's job. Well, not *only* his job. He liked Jerrod, and he hoped his feelings were returned. The last thing he wanted was for him and Peter to get hurt again. He climbed into his car, figuring he'd head home, but his vehicle seemed to have a mind of its own, and he found himself outside Jerrod's rental. He got out and was about to knock when the front door opened and Peter stuck his head out. "I seed you coming."

"Yeah, you did? Is your dad home?" Of course he was if Peter was home.

Peter stepped back and held the door, then closed it hard behind him. "Daddy is upstairs in the shower." He hurried over to the stairs. "Daddy, Mr. Chase is here." He began climbing the stairs. "I told him you were in the bathroom."

Chase snickered as he imagined Jerrod's reaction to that.

Peter came back downstairs and sat on the floor at the coffee table, returning to his coloring.

"What did he say?" Chase asked.

"That it's not nice to say he was in the bathroom. But that's where Daddy is. He said I was supposed to say he was insposed." He shook his head as if to say grown-ups were weird. Chase watched him select his next color, trying not to chuckle. Sometimes kids truly did say the strangest—and most honest—things.

"Do you mean indisposed?"

"Yes. In the bathroom," Peter said, and Chase figured he had gotten as much out of him as he was going to.

"Okay." He leaned over. "What are you coloring?"

"Dinosaurs. Daddy got me the book," he answered without looking up. "I like the red ones." Peter's tongue stuck out from between his teeth as he concentrated.

"Are you being good?" Jerrod asked as he came down the stairs, his hair still wet, a smile on his lips.

"Yes, Daddy. I'm working."

"He did a good job of seeing that I wasn't left all alone." Chase stood, and Jerrod came right over.

"I'm glad you're here. The police called, and Red is apparently stopping over this evening. He seems to have found something and has some questions. I was hoping he might have some answers." Jerrod paused and looked into his eyes. "You know why he's coming, don't you?" Chase sighed and nodded. "And it isn't good."

"They aren't accusing you of anything, if that's what you're thinking. But Hayden and I found out some things today that we turned over to Red." Chase wanted to tell Jerrod all of it, but he was afraid to step into what was now a police investigation. "I think I have to let him fill you in." It felt like he was keeping secrets from Jerrod, but this was official, and he needed to take a step back.

"I see. Does this have anything to do with what happened today?" Jerrod asked.

Chase shrugged. "I wish I knew. I'm hoping that Red will know more than I do." A knock on the door startled them both, and Jerrod answered it. Chase expected Red, so he was surprised when Gizelle barreled inside.

"You really don't get the message, do you?" Jerrod asked, standing between her and Peter, his hands on his hips. "I don't know why you're here, but you need to go."

"I'm appealing the decision, and the court isn't going to let you keep me away from him. So you better figure out what you're going to do when they change their minds." She drew closer to Jerrod, who shook his head. "And you're going to have to argue why I should be kept away."

"Fine, but keep away from us until that happens. Now please leave." Jerrod opened the door. Red stood on the stoop in full uniform. Gizelle's eyes widened, and her mouth hung open. "I suggest you go now." Chase stepped out of the way as Gizelle turned and left the house without another word.

Jerrod let Red in and closed the door.

"Why do I feel like I just stepped into some kind of drama?"

"Because you did. That is my ex-sister-in-law. She's Peter's bio mother, and she abandoned him before my brother died. Her parental rights were terminated before I got custody of him. Now she's decided to return, and she doesn't seem to understand that she can't just walk in whenever she wants. Thank you for helping me get rid of her with a minimum of fuss. She's still under the delusion that she has rights to him, and now she's appealing the termination order, which is one more thing to add to all the drama." Jerrod kept his voice light, probably because of Peter, but Chase heard the underlying tension, and he wondered how much more Jerrod could take. This had to be adding up to a huge burden.

"Are you a real policeman?" Peter asked, standing up and approaching Red with a look of complete awe. "Did you hurt your face chasing a bad guy?"

"Peter," Jerrod chastised.

"It's okay. No, I was in an accident, and I got hurt really bad. Though if I make a scowly face, it does scare the bad guys." Red scowled and narrowed his eyes.

To Chase's surprise, Peter giggled. "You're not that scary, and policemans are good. My teacher at school last year told us so." He looked at Jerrod. "Are you here to help Daddy and me?"

"I'm going to try," Red said gently.

"Okay." Peter returned to the coffee table.

Chase sat down with him. "I'll stay in here so you and Jerrod can talk. Maybe Peter will let me color with him." Peter tapped the page next to his. Chase settled in to color, wishing he could hear what was being said.

CHAPTER 10

"SO MY house isn't the first?" Jerrod asked. He tried to stay quiet so he didn't alarm Peter.

"No. We are still running down some details, but apparently the previous times this was seen, the business owner was shaken down. They refuse to pay, and then their business goes up in smoke. That was a little while ago. What I want to know is if you were pressured not to bid on a job or warned to stay away by anyone."

Jerrod paused to think. "I don't remember anything. I heard about the chance to bid on the condo project through West Electric. Kurt there told me about it, and I looked up the bid details. I worked hard on the bid and then submitted it and was chosen." It seemed pretty straightforward to him.

"Did anyone know you were bidding?" Red asked as he made notes.

Jerrod shook his head. "I don't go around advertising my business. Loose lips sink ships and all that. There are guys who advertise everything they're doing. Not me. I thought the job was something I could do well, and I arranged for two other guys I've worked with in the past to help. Do you really think someone tried to put me out of business by burning me out?"

"We aren't sure. I'll be speaking to the general contractor and the owner of the development to see if they have received any threats or anything. But I wanted to start with you." Red sat patiently while Jerrod thought.

"Now that you mention it.... No. It can't be."

"Please take your time," Red said.

"Three weeks or so before the fire, Peter was with the sitter, and I went to have a drink at Café Belgie. I like the Belgian ales they have on tap. I usually just walk over, and as I was on my way there, I passed some of the guys from Waverly Construction. They congratulated me on getting the contract, and we talked for maybe a minute. Just general pleasantries and then we moved on." Jerrod paused. "The only reason I remember it at all is because it made me uncomfortable, like their words and actions didn't match. After a while, I guess it just faded to the back of my mind. I mean, construction guys can be a hard lot, and I saw them around at some point on one of the job sites."

"Do you know their names?" Red asked, and Jerrod shook his head.

"I think one of them is Sam, but they aren't people I spend time with. Mostly just faces I've seen around sometimes. I wish I could give you more information. As far as I know, Waverly isn't the general contractor on the condo job."

"They are not," Red said. "But apparently word on the street is that Waverly was outbid by AR Construction, and I've been hearing that the Waverly folks are none too happy about it."

Jerrod leaned closer. "All I can say is that I would never let Waverly anywhere near my house. They don't do good work and are always looking for ways to cut corners. If I were you, I'd check with the codes department at borough hall. I bet they can give you a heck of a lot of information on those guys." Red made even more notes. "Part of the reason I bid on the condo job was because it was with AR. They're good people, and the two men who started it have worked hard all their lives, and they built that business from the ground up. They're solid people who give their clients their money's worth. That's why that team is always working."

"And it's also a reason why others might be jealous or want them out of the way," Red submitted, and Jerrod had to agree. "Thank you."

"I hope I was helpful," Jerrod said as he stood up. Red did the same, and they left the kitchen and returned to the living room, where Peter and Chase were having some kind of coloring race. Chase and Peter looked up.

"I think mine is better," Peter said, putting down his crayon as an alarm dinged. "I used more colors."

"Hey. You were only supposed to use three," Chase said in mock outrage before reaching across the table and tickling Peter until his laughter filled the room. Chase let Peter go, setting him on his feet. "Did you get the answers you needed?"

"I think I got the answers I was expecting, which is helpful." Red turned to Jerrod and handed him a card. "If you think of anything else, please let me know."

"Will you be in touch if you find anything?" Jerrod asked.

"If I can," Red said and strode to the door.

"Thank you," Jerrod told him, and he let Red out before closing the door. "Well, I suppose that could have been worse. But this whole situation just got even more convoluted. Now it seems that the fire may be part of some plan to not only stop me, but to hurt the general contractor on the condo project. What the heck is going on?" He lifted Peter into his arms, holding him for comfort.

"Daddy," Peter said as he squirmed to get down. "Was the policeman bad?"

"No. He was trying to help." He set him down again, and Peter hurried upstairs. "I'm not sure what to do right now. What if some local mob is trying to warn me off? What do I do? I have to work, but I can't have my clients put in danger by these thugs."

"Did you tell Red about what happened today?"

Jerrod shook his head. "I didn't think about it. He had his questions, and I answered them. I think it was just kids. None of them were familiar, but Mrs. G told me she would know them if she saw them again, and you do not want to get on her bad side. Not that I know what I'm going to do now other than watch and do whatever I have to in order to keep Peter safe." That was his main concern.

Chase wrapped Jerrod in his arms, holding him. Jerrod closed his eyes and rested his head on Chase's shoulder, trying not to shake like a leaf. "I know, this whole situation sucks."

"The only good thing about it is that I met you. The rest is terrible. I don't know what to do next. Do I just quit and hole up here?"

Chase backed away, locking his intense gaze on Jerrod's. "No. You continue to go out and make a living. You watch the people around you. And most important, you call me or Red if you see anything out of the ordinary. If there are people going around trying to intimidate others, then we need to put a stop to it, or else other people's homes are going to be burned, and who knows what else. The people behind this are total shits." He leaned closer and took Jerrod's breath away with a single kiss. "Never let the assholes win. There are plenty of them in this world, but we have to keep each other safe and stop the jerks from getting what they want. These people don't care who they hurt—you, Peter, or anyone else. All they care about is that they get what they want."

"So I put myself out there and see if they come at me?"

Chase shook his head. "You live your life with your head held high and don't let them intimidate you." This was easier said than done. But Chase was right and he needed to try.

"I have a couple of jobs for tomorrow," Jerrod said.

"Then park in an easily seen spot and watch your truck. Make sure that there are others around if possible, and don't take any chances." Chase lowered his voice. "I don't want anything to happen to you or Peter."

"I know, and I don't want to back down. But it's hard when the person you're up against is in the shadows and could be almost anyone. But you're right. I need to stand up for myself and move forward." Chase held Jerrod again. "At least I'm not alone."

"What do your parents think about all this?"

Jerrod quivered. "My mother told me the last time I spoke to her that Peter and I should leave town and move closer to them. With the house gone, she said there's little tying us here and that we could start over fresh. It was tempting, especially with Gizelle hanging around again. But this is my home, and I want Peter to grow up here. This is where his father intended to raise him, and I want to do the best for Peter that I can."

"Still, it must be hard."

Jerrod shrugged. "Mom is just scared for us, and I can't blame her. She thinks that Gizelle is behind all this and that she should be put in a straightjacket and locked up for the rest of her life."

"I see. So they don't get along."

"Nope. Never did. Mom hated Gizelle on sight. She made an effort while Johnny was still married to her for his sake, but as soon as he separated from her, the claws came out and Gizelle was persona non grata. That's one thing we could always count on about Mom. She could be a tiger when someone was hurting one of us. And Gizelle really tied Johnny up in knots. It was terrible the way she treated him. He kept records of everything she did for months in order to prove that he should have custody, and then once she disappeared and walked away from her responsibilities, he had had enough and petitioned to have her rights terminated. Since she never responded, the court ruled in his favor. I always wondered if she didn't care or simply couldn't be bothered."

"So why did she show up now? It seems rather coincidental to me, and I don't believe in coincidences. She's tied to all this somehow. I just know it."

"Maybe you're right, but I can't think how," Jerrod said softly as another knock sounded on the door.

"What is this, Grand Central Station today?" Chase teased and released him. Jerrod got the door.

A man with a clipboard stood outside. "I have a delivery for Jerrod Whipkey."

"You have the right place," Jerrod said.

The man turned to the back of the truck. He and another man brought in a mattress and box spring set that they carried upstairs. Jerrod followed and showed them where to set it up. After the mattress, they carried in a sofa and end table and the lamp he had picked out. The delivery guys set the sofa on the main wall in the living room, and Peter jumped right up on it.

"No shoes on the furniture," Jerrod scolded lightly. "This is new, and we need to keep it nice."

"Okay, Daddy," Peter said, then took off his shoes and stood on the sofa to bounce.

Jerrod caught him at the second jump. "No. You need to be good. No jumping. The sofa is for sitting."

Peter looked at him. "But you only said no shoes."

Chase snickered from beside him and turned away, probably so Peter didn't see him laughing.

"You need to be good and listen, okay? No shoes, jumping, drawing, or eating on the sofa. Please be good so we can have a few nice things." At least the insurance company had started to come through with some cash for him to replace household items. That had been a big start. "Now go up to your room and play for a while."

"I'm hungry," he said, sticking out his belly. "It's empty."

Jerrod pulled up Peter's shirt and blew a raspberry on his belly, getting giggles. "We'll have dinner soon." He set Peter down, and he hurried up the stairs. The delivery men finished placing things and gathered the packing they'd pulled off the furniture. Jerrod signed their delivery slip and thanked them before seeing them out and closing the door. "At least now this is starting to feel a little more like a home." He had a sofa, chairs, a few tables, a bed, and even a dining table of sorts. The kitchen was mostly mismatched things, but it was functional and filled their needs.

"That it is," Chase said, and Jerrod sat on the new sofa, leaving room for Chase, who joined him. "You know, these are some of my favorite pieces of furniture."

Jerrod smirked. "And why is that?"

Chase leaned closer. "Didn't you ever make out on the sofa when your parents were gone?"

Jerrod rolled his eyes. "Not really. The sofa we had was right in the front room, and there were windows that went all the way down to the floor. Most of the time it felt like a fishbowl, so I stayed away as much as I could. Mom and Dad didn't seem to mind, but I didn't like it. So nope, no couch making out. How about you?"

"I did it with a girl once." Chase drew closer. "Let's just say that it didn't go very well. She was nice and she was willing, but it just didn't feel right to me. I had very little clue about myself back then, but I had these feelings that didn't go away. I thought acting like the other guys would make me be like them, but as you know, that doesn't work. I messed around with Anita some, but after that, I kept to myself."

"So your couch make-out experience is limited," Jerrod said, relieved for some reason. Maybe it was the fact that Chase had gone through a lot of the same things that he had. Jerrod knew what it was like not to feel like he fit in.

"Yeah, it is." He leaned closer, sliding his around Jerrod's neck, drawing him in. "But I think we have a chance to make up for that."

"Daddy. I want dinner, please," Peter said, and they both pulled back.

"Maybe later," Jerrod huffed. "What do you want?"

"Rolly tacos," Peter answered.

Jerrod got up and went to the kitchen, where he heated up the air fryer, another of his recent purchases. Chase joined him a few minutes later. Once it beeped, Jerrod put the taquitos in the basket and slid it into place.

"I know we eat way too much quick food, but…."

"I get it," Chase said. "I don't cook for myself a lot either. But you do have a backyard, and we could arrange to set up a grill. I cook a mean burger and hot dogs. We could have a picnic out there sometime." He shook his head slowly. "Sorry, I shouldn't have just assumed that I could make invitations to your home."

"No. It's great. We could do that. Peter likes that sort of thing, and maybe we could invite some of the other people who have helped us. Hayden and his family, maybe Red, some of the people from the firehouse who pitched in, and a few clients. They've done so much, and I'd like to be able to thank them."

"Okay. Set a date, and I'll help get invitations out to people." Chase leaned against the counter, tugging Jerrod into his arms. "You really are pretty special."

"So are you," Jerrod whispered. "But I can't help wondering if I'm not dragging you into my mess. Look at all this. I thought that my house burned, and now it turns out someone set fire to it and that it could all be part of some bigger conspiracy to try to take over the construction business in this area. Are you sure I'm worth all this trouble? You might be better off to just walk away."

Chase stood taller. "I don't just walk away when things get tough. That's part of being a fireman."

"Yeah, but I don't want to be just part of your job."

"Things regarding you stopped being about my job some time ago. But my job is a big part of who I am, though there are times that I wish I could turn it off. And I'm not going to turn my back because the going gets a little tough. I want you to know that." He drew even closer. Jerrod held his breath as Chase kissed him gently at first, but the heat quickly built between them.

"Is dinner ready?" Peter asked.

Jerrod pulled back before he came into the room. "Just about." All he could think about was the fact that there was a brand-new bed upstairs and that he was more than ready to break it in. He held Chase's gaze for a few seconds before the timer went off on the air fryer, indicating that dinner, such as it was, was ready.

CHAPTER 11

As WITH any meal with Peter and Jerrod, dinner was interesting and involved a lot of Peter talking about anything and everything. And the kid did definitely love his rolly tacos. Not that Chase minded. It was almost like being part of the family. When they were done, Chase took things to the sink, setting the last of the dishes in it as his phone rang. He suppressed a sigh when he saw his mother's name.

"I'll take this out back," he said softly, as though his mother could hear, and went out into the small yard. "Hey, Mom."

"You are alive," she snipped. "It's been weeks since I heard anything from you. I was starting to think you had died in one of your fires and that no one had told me or your father."

He groaned softly. She had always been overly dramatic where he was concerned. His mother had a successful career managing boutiques for one of the large retail chains that sold makeup and jewelry. At one point she had twenty managers under her. There was nothing that she couldn't handle when it came to her stores. But with him, everything was absolutely over the top. "I'm fine, Mom, as you can hear. I'm having dinner with a friend and his son tonight."

"What sort of friend? Is he divorced? I'm assuming that since he has children, he isn't the kind of friend that you would be in a relationship with."

Chase turned away from the house. "Never make assumptions, Mom. I met Jerrod through work, and he's raising his nephew." More than anything, he hated the road this conversation was taking. "Was there a reason you called other than to give me grief?" The best way to get to his mom was to call her on her drama. That usually helped get her to the heart of the matter.

"I called because I was worried," she told him.

"Okay, but I'm fine now. How are you and Dad?" Chase asked, and his mother brought him up to date on all the happenings in their community, including gossip about people Chase had never met and didn't know from Adam.

"Your father has taken up tennis and is trying to get me to play with him. Can you imagine me in one of those short skirts with my legs? Please. I don't need anyone to know that I spent years walking on concrete floors and that my legs look like purple caterpillars made tracks all over them." He could almost see her shaking her head at the notion.

"I think it's a great idea. Not the legs part, but playing tennis. I think it's something you'd be good at." He had no particular reason why, other than she had always been good at sports and outdoor activities.

"Me? No."

"Yeah. Remember Little League? Dad tried to help me, but it was you who spent the time after school playing catch with me. I say go for it, and if you get the chance, wipe the floor with them." He smiled, and she laughed. It was a good sound.

"I'll think about it." She sighed, and the lightheartedness that had taken over seemed to fly away on the summer breeze. "You need to settle down, you know."

"Geez, Mom, you're giving me conversational whiplash here." He turned and peered in the window to where Jerrod lifted Peter, the two of them playing airplane or something. In a few seconds, they were out of sight. "And things will happen when the time is right."

She hummed in that way she had that always drove him crazy. Like she knew better than he did. "With the man raising his nephew? You know kids are hard and take commitment. Though I do like the idea of a grandson. He could call me Nana—"

"Hold on. Don't get ahead of yourself here. Jerrod is…." He paused, but he needed to get his mother off this particular track. "He's a great man, but he's going through a lot right now."

"So you aren't serious?" she asked, and Chase wished he knew if she was excited or guarded. Sometimes it was hard to tell.

"I like him, Mom. But there's a lot going on in his life right now. I think he likes me too, but with all the background noise, it's hard to cut through it. I can tell you that I see them a couple times a week and we do stuff like have dinner, and I color with Peter." He paused. "But…." He swallowed hard.

"Oh for heaven's sake, just let the other shoe drop and tell me."

"I met them when I saved Peter from a fire at their house," Chase said. "I got him out of the burning building. So are Jerrod's feelings real or is he sort of grateful for what I did? I don't think that's what it is, but it's hard to be sure."

His mother tsked. "Just kiss him. You'll know then."

"I have."

"And you're still unsure? Is he a sucky kisser or something?" He could almost see the amusement on her face.

"Mom," Chase chastised. "And no, he isn't. Not at all. Jerrod is…. He's really…." He couldn't even finish the thought, she had him so turned around. Or maybe it was Jerrod who had him all wound up. He smiled, looking through the window as Jerrod peered out at him. "He's watching me."

"Of course he is," his mom said. "And you got all dreamy for a second there."

"Gee, thanks."

"Look, all I can tell you is to understand how you feel and then talk to him. It isn't that hard, but you can tie yourself in knots trying to figure someone out when all it takes are words—something the male of the species seems to have trouble with. Lord knows your father did. That man would run a marathon with three lions chasing him the entire way before he'd ever willingly talk about his feelings with anyone." Sometimes she really had a way with words.

"Tell me about it." Most of the time, the best Chase got was a humph and a pat on the back.

"Then don't act like him," his mom said.

"I don't," Chase protested.

"Right." His mom could out-sarcasm any teenager. "That's why you're telling me about all this rather than him. There aren't some magic words. Just talk to him." He could tell she was smiling again. "And for the record, I'd say that it's about time you found someone. Maybe you can think about settling down."

"Okay, Mom. I think it's time for me to go. I don't want to be rude, but I'll call you later."

"Fine. As long as I don't have to wait another three weeks." She ended the call, and Chase rolled his eyes. She always had to get the last word. He put his phone back in his pocket and returned to where Jerrod was finishing up in the kitchen.

Every time Chase came over, the house looked a little more like a home. The walls were still bare, but the small table now had placemats and a napkin holder in the center. "You're really starting to get things together here."

"Yeah. With the police indicating that I'm not a suspect in the fire, the insurance company is starting to move forward. They're sending me a bunch of forms so I can list the contents of the house. That ought to be fun." He pulled out a chair and sat at the table. "But I suppose it's how they do things." He sighed softly. "At least I had replacement value on everything."

Chase took the other chair, gently putting his hand on Jerrod's. "Have they given you an indication of a time frame?"

"They said it won't be too long for the personal property portion of the claim. The rest will take time because the insurance company wants to repair the house because they think it will be cheaper, but I don't think the borough is going to allow that. Until someone makes a decision, though, we're going to wait."

Chase lightly squeezed Jerrod's hand. "The guys tell me that it usually takes about a year or so to rebuild. I know that probably isn't what you wanted to hear."

Jerrod nodded slowly. "I think I knew that, but it's been hard to think too far ahead. At least I have a place for Peter and me. The landlord has been really cooperative. I think the whole thing with letting Gizelle in the house has him spooked, because he sent a letter of apology and indicated that we could use the house for as long as we needed it. He also said that he had some electrical jobs in a couple of his properties and asked if I was interested in the work. So at least things are starting to look up."

"And how is Peter doing? I mean, are there any lasting effects on him?"

"I think it's too soon to tell. He's sleeping through the night, so that's a good thing. I keep hoping he doesn't have nightmares about it. But then I tend to think you've helped a lot with that." He turned his hand, and their fingers entwined.

"I'm glad I could help," Chase said softly, looking into Jerrod's eyes. Damn, he could get lost in them as they drew him closer. He leaned over the table, and Jerrod did the same.

"You've been a huge help to both of us, and I don't know how I can thank you." His eyes grew darker, green flecks dancing in azure. "I've been thinking about you a lot when you aren't here."

"Me too," Chase whispered. "But I don't want to push in or anything."

Jerrod squeezed his fingers. "You haven't been. I don't know where we'd be without everything you've done." Jerrod parted his lips, and all Chase could think about was tasting them, taking Jerrod until he was breathless. Hell, he wanted to throw Jerrod over his shoulder, carry him up to that new bed of his, and break it in properly until Jerrod was hoarse from passion.

"Daddy, can we do something?" Peter asked from the other room.

Jerrod straightened up but didn't pull his hand away. "What do you want to do? It will be time to go to bed soon."

Peter came into the kitchen, holding a stuffed duck. "I don't know. I'm bored." His shoulders slumped, and he had all the dejection of one of the orphans from *Annie*. "I don't know what to do."

"Well, maybe you could color for a while. Or I could see if I could find some cartoons on the computer." Jerrod released Chase's hand and lifted Peter into his arms, heading for the other room. It wasn't long before Jerrod had Peter settled on the sofa with a laptop on the coffee table. Jerrod closed the curtains and turned out the lights, making the room dark and soothing. Then he got a light blanket and put it over Peter's legs.

"I have to give him a chance to wind down," Jerrod said quietly, turning down the kitchen lights so there was just the one over the table.

"I suppose. He tends to go a mile a minute."

"He does. My mother told me I should get him something for his hyperactivity…." He frowned.

Chase was surprised. "He's curious, and he asks a lot of questions. That doesn't mean he needs medication."

"To my mother it does. The last time we visited, she told Peter that he was talking back to her when all he was doing was asking questions. I think it got under her skin a little. She loves Peter and is thrilled to have a grandchild, but I think Mom prefers him in small doses and doesn't understand that Peter is smarter than her—or me, for that matter. In the fall he's supposed to be in first grade, but when I spoke to the school about the kinds of things they will cover, Peter is already reading at the second-grade level, and he can add numbers in his head faster than I can. The school is going to put him in first grade but have special sessions with him for the things he excels at. I want him to learn to be around other kids his own age." Jerrod scratched the back of his head. "I don't want to hold him back, but…."

"You aren't. Let him be around kids his own age for a while. You can decide what you want at the end of the school year. Maybe he switches to third grade instead of second."

"I know. I'm hoping that in his own way, Peter will tell me what I should do." He sighed and rested his head on the table.

Chase brought his chair around, sat next to him, and gathered Jerrod into his arms.

"I never expected to become a parent. I always thought that since I was gay, it was something that wouldn't be open to me. When Johnny asked me to be guardian of Peter if anything happened to him, I thought it was one of those 'it will never happen' kinds of things." Jerrod had said that before, but Chase figured he needed the outlet. "Now I can't imagine not being a parent."

"I think I can understand that."

Jerrod lifted his gaze. "You know that no matter what, Peter has to be the first and most important thing in my life, right?"

Chase gently stroked Jerrod's jaw. "Of course." That seemed like a no-brainer.

"I dated this guy, Barry, maybe six months after Johnny died, and he couldn't understand why I didn't just get a sitter every time he wanted to go to Harrisburg to the clubs or out on a Saturday night for drinks. I'm ashamed to say that I did it a few times until I realized that I was missing out on time with Peter. He's only going to be little once." He swallowed as Chase sighed and waited for him to continue.

When he didn't, Chase prompted, "What happened?"

"Peter was four, and I came home and he ran into the living room to show me how he could tie his shoes. It was late, but he had been waiting up for me and had to show me. Barry stood there behind me and grew impatient while Peter demonstrated this great feat that he'd mastered. And once Peter was done, Barry humphed and asked if the kid was going to bed already."

Chase felt tension building in Jerrod's shoulders. "What a real—" He stopped himself before swearing. "Jerk."

Jerrod nodded. "I told him that I was taking Peter up to bed. Then I lifted my son in my arms and climbed the stairs. 'Good night, Barry. I'm sure you can close the door behind you.'" Jerrod smirked.

"You didn't say that." Chase found himself smiling.

"I did, and he actually had the gall to call me the next afternoon. I simply told him then that I didn't think that I had any time for dating and he would probably be better off finding someone else." Jerrod leaned closer. "He was really angry and began calling me names and saying that Peter would be better off with my parents. I simply ended the call." He sighed softly. "I did like him. Barry was fun, and he was amazing between the sheets."

Chase's cheeks heated, and he chuckled softly to himself. "He was, huh?"

Jerrod nodded. "Oh yeah. But that and dancing was all he had. Barry could strut better than John Travolta in *Saturday Night Fever*. He knew his strengths, and he used them to his advantage. But in every other manner, he was selfish and put himself first. It took me too long to realize that spending time with him wasn't worth missing important things like Peter learning to tie his shoes or picking up a book and reading out loud for the first time. I missed some of those, but I won't do that again." Jerrod got up and checked in the other room. "I'll be right back."

Jerrod left the room and spoke quietly to Peter, and then Chase heard the stairs creak. He knew it would be a few minutes before Jerrod returned, so he went into the living room, folded the blanket, and straightened things up, putting away the crayons before settling on the sofa, leaning back. He closed his eyes and let contentment wash over him.

"You okay?" Jerrod asked, surprising Chase a little. He hadn't meant to doze off.

"Sure. I was just waiting for you. Is Peter asleep?"

"Yeah. He went out like a light. He plays so hard and doesn't stop until he crashes completely. Then it's quiet and I get a few hours. Hopefully he'll sleep through the night and won't be up at six in the morning ready to go. There are many times I wish he'd learn to sleep in."

"Have you tried putting him to bed later?" Chase asked.

"Doesn't matter. He gets up at the same time and is grumpy for part of the day. As soon as the sun comes through his window, he's up. I tried shades that darkened the room, and that helped for a few days, but then Peter got up, opened the shades, and came to find me." Jerrod smiled. "Maybe he's part rooster or something."

"Maybe. Or he's just one of those people who are happy to greet the morning." Chase leaned closer. "Maybe Peter is just happy, and he looks forward to the day. Most of us seem to be happiest once it's over." Chase stood. "I can tell you that at the moment, I'm pretty happy that today is over, but the night, well, that's just begun." He watched those amazing eyes, wondering whether Jerrod was going to take his hint or if he was going to tell Chase it was time for him to leave.

CHAPTER 12

PETER WAS asleep, and Jerrod wanted nothing more than to take Chase up on his offer. But he hesitated, wondering if this was the right thing to do. Maybe it would be best to wait.... Jerrod shook his head and groaned to himself. What was he holding out for? Until Peter was a teenager? He smiled at himself, and Chase released his hand. "I'll call you tomorrow," he said softly.

"No," Jerrod said.

Chase's eyebrows slid upward. "You don't want me to call?"

"No. I mean, yes. I mean that I don't want you to go." He was really messing this up. "It's been a while, and after the last time, I figured that I'd have to wait until Peter was older before I could date and have… you know… that kind of life again. And now here you are, and things feel so different this time." He extended his hand, and Chase took it again. He smiled and squeezed his fingers before turning out the lights and checking the door. Once he was sure the house was secure, he led Chase up the stairs and past Peter's room to his sparse bedroom, then closed the door.

As soon as the latch caught, he sighed and lost some of his nervousness. He locked the door and turned back to Chase, who stood beside the bed. Jerrod just watched him for a few moments before stepping closer. Chase took him in his arms, crushing him against his chest as he kissed Jerrod with a force he didn't know was possible—one that carried him away. Responsibility, worry, and all thoughts of anything outside the bedroom flew from his mind as Chase's lips took him on a journey he didn't think could ever happen, and they still had all their clothes on.

Chase was a take-charge man, and that quickly became apparent. Chase guided Jerrod down onto the bed, their gazes holding as Chase worked open the buttons of Jerrod's shirt, the air conditioning gliding over his skin as soon as the fabric fell to his sides. Chase kissed him again as Jerrod tugged at the hem of his shirt, pulling it upward until Chase backed up just enough for Jerrod to get his shirt off. Chase's golden skin glistened in the soft moonlight coming in through the windows. He cupped Chase's cheeks, whisker stubble rough against his palms.

"Do you know how stunning you are?" Chase asked in a soft, deep voice that sent ripples of desire rushing through Jerrod.

"Me?" Jerrod said. "You're like some firefighting god." He drew Chase closer, their lips coming together once more. Jerrod easily lost himself in the sensation, kicking off his shoes as Chase did the same. He wanted more of Chase, running his hands down his muscular back and over the curve of his superior ass. Some guys had a butt, but this.... Jerrod squeezed the muscularly hard cheeks. This was an ass of epic proportions. He squeezed again, and Chase moaned softly against his lips.

"A god, huh?" Chase whispered when he pulled back.

"Don't let it go to your head," Jerrod retorted, working open Chase's belt and then the top button of his jeans. The rest of the buttons popped open behind it, and Jerrod slid the denim down, taking the briefs along with them, Chase's thick cock bursting out. He stroked the length while Chase lolled his head back.

"The things you do to me," Chase groaned softly, kissing Jerrod once more as he slipped the jeans down past Chase's hips.

Jerrod held those perfect asscheeks, his fingers digging into the smooth flesh. Then he gathered Chase to him, chests pressed together, heat building between them. Chase shimmied out of his jeans and climbed off the bed. The man was Greek-statue-worthy as the moonlight shone off his golden skin—wide shoulders, narrow waist—but it was his eyes, dark and brimming with passion, that took Jerrod's breath away. Chase tugged at Jerrod's pants, and Jerrod got them over his hips. Chase pulled them off his legs and dropped the fabric to the floor.

His underwear followed. "I like you this way," Chase whispered.

"What, kind of full in the middle and wondering when middle age is going to hit?"

Chase rolled his eyes. "No. Just like this. Beautiful, naked, and all mine." He climbed back onto the bed, covering Jerrod with his body, the heat building once more. This was what Jerrod dreamed about at night when he was alone, but it seemed his imagination was lacking when it came to the real thing. "I want you, Jerrod."

"Then take me."

And Chase did, right between those luscious lips and all the way to the root in a breath-stealing move that sent Jerrod's eyes rolling to the back of his head.

"Oh God," Jerrod moaned as Chase surrounded him in wet heat. He closed his eyes, letting the sensation wash over him. "What are you doing to me?"

Chase pulled back. "I thought what's-his-name was really good in bed?" His eyes danced. "Didn't he make you fly?"

Jerrod shook his head. "Not like that. He had other talents, but then maybe my point of reference isn't as broad as it could be."

Chase patted his hip gently. "Don't you dare apologize for something like that, because that only means you haven't met someone who was willing to get to know *you*." He kissed away Jerrod's meager protest before sucking a trail down his chest, then engulfing him once more.

Jerrod wasn't sure how much longer he could take this. The energy built inside him, and he clutched the bedding as he tried to remain in control, but Chase seemed to know what he wanted before he did. "Chase...." Just when Jerrod thought he was about to tumble over the edge, Chase pulled away. Jerrod growled and whimpered, breathing deeply as he tried to think. "You really are evil."

"I don't want this to be over too soon." Chase climbed onto the bed, pulling Jerrod into an embrace.

"I know. But...."

Chase chuckled slightly. "You and I have all night. There's no need to rush. And sometimes anticipation makes everything better."

Jerrod rested his head on Chase's shoulder, running his fingers over his chest, the muscle flexing slightly under his touch. He smiled slightly, tweaking one of Chase's pink nipples, earning a soft moan. "I see. You like that."

"Yeah," Chase said, and Jerrod leaned closer, running his tongue over the tightening bud before sucking lightly.

"Okay." He sucked harder, loving the soft sounds Chase made. It was gratifying that he could get Chase to quiver under him. That was a rush. Jerrod was well aware that he was not the kind of guy who turned heads. He worked hard, and that helped keep the weight off and stuff, but with Peter, he didn't have the time for everything. The gym had fallen by the wayside years ago, and quick meals had replaced thoughtful homecooked items. But the fact that he could get hunky Chase to react to him with breathless abandon was incredible.

"Damn," Chase whimpered. "You make me want things that I never thought possible." He grabbed Jerrod, crushing them together in a strong hug, kissing him deeply. Jerrod lost himself in the moment, letting the heat and passion build.

Chase rocked slowly above him, and Jerrod moved right along with him, holding Chase's ass, loving the flex of the muscles as they moved together. Energy built between them as Jarrod held Chase, looking into his eyes, the two of them alone in the moment of building ecstasy that never seemed to end… until Chase drove him to the brink and over the edge.

Jerrod lay on the covers, a sweaty mess, holding Chase in his arms, eyes closed, just enjoying the moment.

"Daddy." A knock followed the cry, and Jerrod instantly tensed.

"What is it, buddy?" he asked. "You should be in bed."

"Okay, Daddy. But there's someone knocking on the door downstairs. I'll go get it."

Jerrod jumped out of bed, pulling on his jeans as he grabbed his underwear, using it to wipe himself up. He put on his shirt as he opened the door, then raced downstairs. "I got it, Peter," Jerrod said as the knock sounded once more. He lifted Peter into his arms, peering out the window to try to see who it was. Then he opened the door partway. "Can I help you?"

"There's smoke coming from the back," the young man said. "Should I call the fire department?"

"Yes." Jerrod set Peter down and told him to stay right there. Then he raced through the house to the back to pull open the door. He half expected an inferno climbing the rear of the house, but instead he saw nothing but a bright dancing glow until he approached the back fence, where the neighbor behind him had set up a bonfire, probably to try to burn the trash and yard waste rather than disposing of it properly. The flames reached four feet in the air. He went back inside and told the young man who stood in the front doorway what was happening.

"Thanks. So it's in the yard of the house directly behind this address?" the young man said, relating the details on the call.

Jerrod nodded. "Apparently it's someone burning yard waste or something."

The young man relayed the information before waving and heading off down the sidewalk.

Jerrod closed the door and locked it.

"Is everything okay? Is the fire going to come get us?" Peter asked, fear in his voice.

"No," he answered as Chase came down the stairs.

"The department is on their way," Chase said, shaking his head. "That is not allowed in the borough."

Sirens sounded, and Jerrod turned out the lights and took Peter back up the stairs. He got him tucked in bed and sat with him until the activity behind the house died down. "It's okay. The fire is out now." He rubbed Peter's back until he rolled over, holding his stuffed duck.

Jerrod left the room, closing the door partway, then met Chase in the bedroom. "What the hell were they thinking?" he whispered. Things had finally quieted down. He went to the window overlooking the backyard, now bright from the firefighters and their equipment, but thankfully the yellow of the flames was no longer to be seen. He pulled the curtains, casting the room in darkness, and sat on the side of the bed.

"All I could think of was making sure we weren't going to get burned out again."

Chase slipped his arms around Jerrod's waist. "Your neighbor is a real idiot, and the ticket he's going to receive should deter him from further late-night bonfires. Plus, once the captain gets done notifying the borough, there will be letters and warnings coming his way."

"I see." Jerrod turned away from the east-facing window, his heart finally beating at a more normal pace. "I don't know how much more of this I can take." He sighed and stripped off his clothes before sliding under the covers. "I just reacted and was ready to grab Peter and run out of the house if the fire had been a real threat. In fact, I don't know why I didn't do that."

"You made sure Peter was safe, and then you checked on the danger," Chase said softly, sliding under the covers next to him. "It turned out that there wasn't an immediate threat. You and Peter are okay."

"Yeah, I know that," Jerrod said with an edge in his voice. "But what am I going to do? What if the next threat isn't as benign?" He sat up. "We have to figure out who is behind all this so that I can sleep at night again. I know tonight is different because something actually happened, but I go to bed and doze on and off all night, waking just in case something happens and I need to be ready to get Peter out. I have a fire extinguisher in every closet in the house and one in the kitchen. I keep thinking that every sound is someone trying to get inside or into the backyard. Last night I stared out the back window downstairs for half an hour after one of the neighbors' dogs started barking. I didn't see anything, but I couldn't go back to sleep either." He closed his eyes. "Maybe I need help."

Chase put his arms around him. "What you need is a chance to get some rest and to let a little time pass. The fire and the loss are still new, and I think it's natural to be jumpy." He gently soothed Jerrod down onto the pillow. "I'm here, and I won't let anything happen to you. Just rest and know that I'm here and you and Peter aren't alone." His voice carried this soothing property, and Jerrod could almost believe him.

"But what if you fall asleep and something happens?"

Chase tugged him tighter. "I've slept at fire stations during my internship and since I've been here. You learn to rest while at the same time be ready at a moment's notice. So trust me. If anything happens, I will be up and ready for both of you. Now roll over."

Jerrod humphed as he turned onto his belly, and then Chase's big, strong hands massaged his back. "Damn…," Jerrod hummed as those amazing hands performed a miracle, letting the tension flow out of him. "That's good." Jerrod closed his eyes and tried to relax. Chase made it easy, and Jerrod groaned softly as Chase's touch swept up and down his back. This wasn't a sexual kind of touch, but it was intimate and caring.

"Breathe deeply, let the tension go," Chase whispered, and Jerrod did his best. He visualized the tension leaving him with each breath, and after a few minutes, his mind went blank and all he felt were Chase's hands on him. Time seemed to have no relevance as Chase worked his magic, and when his touch eased and pulled away, Jerrod lay still as Chase settled next to him and pulled up the covers. "Just rest now."

Jerrod hummed his agreement and closed his eyes, letting sleep overtake him.

Light streamed into the room when he woke. Jerrod blinked himself awake. He actually felt rested as he rolled over to find the other half of the bed empty. He sat up, rubbed his eyes, and got out of bed, wondering if Chase was somewhere in the house, but it seemed silent. He reached for his phone to check the time and started because he really needed to get moving. He was scheduled to be at a job in half an hour. He grabbed clean clothes and pulled them on before heading to Peter's room, where he found his son playing blocks, already dressed—well, his shoes didn't match, but that didn't matter.

"Daddy. You sleeped a long time." He jumped up and ran over. "My tummy is hungry."

"Mine too." He took Peter's hand and led him downstairs, where he made a quick breakfast before getting him ready for day care.

"Where is Mr. Chase?" Peter asked.

"I'm not sure." Jerrod checked his phone and found a message. "He said that he had to go in to work and that he didn't want to wake us up." A bunch of sleepy emojis followed. "He says he'll call later and that he hopes we have a nice day."

"Okay." Peter took a bite of his cereal. "Did you and Mr. Chase have a sleepover?"

Jerrod hesitated, considering how much he wanted to say about his relationship with Chase. He liked him a great deal, and Jerrod could easily see himself falling for him. But still, he hesitated because he didn't want Peter to get too attached. If things didn't work out, the last thing he wanted was for Peter to be hurt as well. Maybe it was already too late for that. Jerrod had no idea. In the end Jerrod decided on honesty… to a degree. "Yes."

Peter took another bite. "Do you like him? Is he your boyfriend?"

That question threw him for a loop for a second. "I don't know. I think he might be. Is that okay?"

Peter nodded. "Yes, Daddy." The tone told him Peter thought he was being silly. "Will I have a boyfriend when I grow up?"

"You might. Or you could have girlfriends. It's okay to love whoever you want to."

Peter raised his gaze. "But you like boys, right?"

Jerrod couldn't believe he was having this conversation. "It isn't important if you like boys or girls as long as you're happy. That's all that counts. I promise you that. The rest is just packaging on the outside. What really counts is what someone is like on the inside. Okay?" He hoped that would be enough of an answer for now. And thankfully Peter seemed satisfied and went back to his breakfast. Jerrod ate quickly and then got everything ready for work before bundling Peter into the truck to drop him off at day care.

"Do you think Mr. Chase will be back? He isn't mad at us, is he?" Peter asked.

"No. He isn't mad, and I hope he'll be back." After last night, Jerrod sure as heck hoped to see him again soon, but with the way things had been going, he hoped it was under happy circumstances rather than in an emergency.

CHAPTER 13

CHASE MADE it through the day without embarrassing himself. He was so tired that as soon as his shift ended, he went right home and collapsed into bed. So when someone pounded on his door a few hours later, he barely heard it. Still, he managed to pull himself out of sleep and answered the door, bleary-eyed.

"Red?" he asked, stepping back. "What's going on? What time is it?"

"About eight at night." He paused for just a moment. "Look, there's been another fire. The department in town responded to it, and when they made their report, it looked enough like the ones we've already seen that I flagged it. The scene is under control and the fire is out. I checked with the captain, and he said that Hayden was out of town on vacation for a few days and suggested that you might want to come along."

Instantly awake, Chase closed the door behind Red and hurried to his room. "Give me five minutes." He checked that he was presentable, then slipped on shoes and socks before rejoining Red in the living room. "I'm ready." He grabbed his wallet and keys before following Red out to his patrol car.

There was still a great deal of activity when they arrived at the house fire scene. Chase got out with Red and approached the captain. "What do we have?" Red asked.

"Possible arson," he answered before turning to Chase.

"He's with me," Red said without explaining further. "Can someone show us what you found?" He had already taken charge, and the captain nodded and led the two of them inside.

"At first we thought this was electrical."

"But then you found melted electrical caps and other debris near the box, but not part of it," Chase supplied. The captain nodded. "We've seen this before in multiple locations, including at the construction location fire a week ago." He knelt, carefully looking over what they had without touching anything. "This looks the same as the fire at Jerrod's house and the one at the condominium construction site." He turned to Red. "Is there any connection?"

"That's what we need to find out. But I wanted to be sure before we went down that road," Red said before making notes and taking photographs. Chase stayed out of the way and let Red do his job. After a few minutes, he took the time to look over the rest of the basement area.

"How did the arsonist get in?" he asked, partially to himself.

"What?" the captain asked while Red stood up.

"This device was planted in here. That I'm pretty sure of. But how did they get in? There isn't any sign of a break-in, so how did it get here? I doubt the owner just let anyone inside the house." He wandered through the basement area. "I never asked that question about Jerrod's place either. Granted, so much of the house was damaged that it would be hard in that case to pinpoint anything."

"True." Red made a few more notes. "We need to speak to the homeowner."

"They're out front. It's a man with three children. They have been near the sidewalk through this whole ordeal. We've contacted the Red Cross, and as far as I know, they are stepping in to help the family for the next few days."

Chase followed Red outside, where they found the family huddled together, the youngest in her father's arms.

"How is our house?" one of the kids asked as the father came forward.

"There's extensive damage," Red said as gently as possible.

The father handed the child to one of her siblings and spoke to them quietly before the three of them stepped away.

"Okay, give it to me straight."

Chase remained quiet and let Red do the talking. "Well, we found the cause of the fire, and I need to ask you some questions. Has there been anyone in the house recently? Workmen? Visitors?"

"What are you trying to say? That someone set the fire?"

Chase nodded. "We believe so, yes."

The man paled and seemed to zone out for a few seconds. "Why would someone do that?"

"We're trying to figure that out," Red said. "But what we don't know is how they got inside."

He shrugged. "I don't know. I mean…," he stammered, and Chase tried to help.

"Did you have any sort of workman in the house? The gas company or anyone like that. Anyone at all?"

The man paused and blinked a few times. "There was a gas leak in the neighborhood a few days ago, and a technician asked to come in so he could check for gas in the house."

"Can you describe him?" Red asked.

The father just shook his head. "I don't remember him, but I have a doorbell camera, and he came to the front door. My computer was in the front room of the house. Do you know if it's okay? I can access the records through it."

"Let me see if I can get to it," Chase said before checking with the captain.

"The fire was mainly in back, so go through the front," the captain answered, and Chase carefully went inside. The room was pretty dry, with most of the department's efforts concentrated on the back of the house. He found the laptop sitting on the coffee table. He unplugged it and brought it out and handed it and the cord to Red, who passed it to the father.

They used the hood of one of the trucks as a makeshift table and lifted the lid, booting up the computer. Thankfully it started with no issues. They had to link it to a phone to get internet service, but they were able to access the doorbell files. "How long do you keep the records?"

The father shrugged. "I don't know. I think up to a week, though it only records when there is activity. I hope things go back far enough." He logged in, and then Red took over. He downloaded the files and then got a drive to save them to.

"You aren't going to look now?" Chase asked.

"It could take a while, and my partner, Carter, is a computer expert. I'll give all of this to him, and if there is anything to find, he'll do it." Red captured copies of all the files and then handed the computer back. "I appreciate your help."

Chase moved away as Red got the information he needed. He wandered around the side of the house, staying away from the others, who were beginning to put their gear away. Chase felt like they were missing something. He looked up and down the building as he moved.

"What are you looking for?" Red asked.

"I don't know," Chase said. "I keep wondering what kind of link there could be to this fire."

Red smiled as they stopped moving. "The father, Gordon Williams, is an HVAC contractor, and guess what one of his contracts was?"

Chase groaned. "No way."

"Yup. He has a small firm with about six guys, and they were gearing up to do all the heat pump installations for the condos once the units were built. Now he's wondering if the project will go ahead at all."

"You think this and Jerrod's fire were messages to stay away?" Chase asked. Red nodded. "I suppose that most people will be able to make the connection, especially in the construction community." He sighed as the full weight of what was happening settled on his shoulders. "How in the hell are we going to find out who is behind this? Are we all putting our lives and homes in danger?" He was worried about Red now. "Do you think they'll come after you?"

Red nodded. "Will you do me a favor and look over my house to make sure nothing has been planted there? We'll also check out Jerrod's new place."

"Good idea," Chase said. "Let's go." He rode with Red to his home on Pomfret Street.

"What's going on?" a man asked as he entered.

"Terry, this is Chase," Red said.

"I know you. I saw you win gold at the Olympics," Chase said, unable to help his huge grin. "Your race was really something." They shook hands, with Chase a little starstruck.

"We need to check the basement," Red said.

"For gas?" Terry asked. "There was a man here from the gas company maybe an hour ago who said there was a leak in the area. He asked to check in the basement."

Chase's heart beat fast as he followed Red to the stairs. "Where is the electrical box? Go back and tell Terry to get out now and call this in." He reached the bottom of the stairs and found the electrical box. He also found a small box up in the trusses nearby. If he hadn't been looking for it, he probably would never have seen it from the way it blended in. It looked like it might be an electrical junction box, except for the zip ties holding it in place.

"I put out the alert," Red said as he came up behind him. "What the hell do we do?"

Case looked around and pulled a lidded plastic tub off a nearby shelf, then dumped the contents on the floor. "Fill that with water. We can immerse it, and maybe that will stop whatever ignition mechanism is inside."

Red dragged the green tub to the washbasin and used the extender hose to start filling it. Chase located a toolbox and found a set of snips to cut the zip ties that held the box in place. "How full is it?"

"About a foot?" Red answered as he continued filling.

Chase slowly reached for the box. He held it steady, his heart racing as he forced himself to stay calm. He snipped first one tie and then the second, hoping like hell this thing didn't go off in his hand. The box came free, and he lowered it carefully before walking back toward Red. Chase wanted to run, but had no idea how motion would affect the device, so he took even, gliding steps until he reached the tub and then set the box on top of the water and let it sink.

Red dropped the hose in the tub, and they took off toward the stairs. They made it about halfway up before a gurgling, hissing sound came from the other room. "Go. Get out now." Chase hoped his little trick would work, but wasn't sure.

They met Terry near the front door as firetrucks began arriving. Chase immediately explained what they'd found to the captain as firefighters raced inside. He and Red kept out of the way, standing on the sidewalk with Terry as lights flashed all around them in the darkness.

Chase pulled out his phone and called Jerrod. "Has someone from the gas company stopped by today?" He found himself breathless with worry.

"No," Jerrod answered. "What's wrong?"

Chase breathed a sigh of relief. "Go to the basement and check to see if there is a small box zip-tied to the rafters anywhere in the area of the junction box. Better yet, get out of the house and take Peter to a restaurant for ice cream or something. I know it's late, but just do it. Then text me where you are." There was no way in hell that he was going to let anything happen to them. "It's just a precaution, but please do this for me."

"Okay. I was just putting Peter to bed," he said, his voice jittery. "Okay. I'm getting him now."

Chase ended the call as some of his colleagues exited the house carrying the green tub, which they set on the sidewalk.

"This is a mess, but good thinking to immerse this thing," one of the second-shift guys said. "I'm Christopher, by the way."

"Chase," he said, shaking hands.

"It obviously went off, but the water put it out before it could get a real hold. You can see that this thing was primed to burn hot." The upper edges of the tub had melted a little. "Don't touch the water. It's damned hot, and we don't know what's in it."

Chase nodded and turned to find Red, who, along with Terry, was answering questions from a set of police officers. He strode over. "We need to get to Jerrod's to see if the house is okay." He hated to interrupt, but their job was only partly done.

"On it," Red said. "Guys, I'll answer your questions when I get to the station. But we have to check on another location."

They got in the police car, turned on the lights, and beat it to Jerrod's. Thankfully, they found nothing. The basement was clear, with no strange boxes lodged in any of the rafters. Chase sent Jerrod a text to let him know and got a response that he and Peter would stay where they were for the moment.

"What a night," Chase said.

"Yeah. But we made some progress. We know how they were getting inside, at least for now."

"But we also know they're getting desperate and bolder. They tried to set fire to your house, which they had to know was going to bring the entire department down on them." Chase paused. "We need to find out who this guy is and get him the hell off the street before someone is killed."

"Hopefully the video will show us something." Red sighed. "Look, I need to get back because the guys are going to be grilling Terry, and I need to be there. Do you want me to drop you off at your place?"

Chase hesitated but then nodded. "Please." He needed to get his truck so he could meet Jerrod and Peter. He figured this was going to be a rough night.

HE WAS right. By the time he got to Jerrod, he was at his wits' end: eyes wide, holding Peter next to him as he sat in the booth of the Italian restaurant. They sat in a room off to the side, a cup of coffee in front of Jerrod and a half-empty cup of Sprite for Peter. "How is it?"

"Everything is fine," Chase said, taking Jerrod's hand. "I just wanted to be sure. I'm sorry if I scared the two of you.' He kept his voice soft. "But I needed to know you were safe."

"Okay," Jerrod said, making no effort to get up. "What was with the gas man?"

Chase sat across from them. "Let's get you both home and Peter in bed. Then I can tell you everything. I have some questions for you as parts of this puzzle begin to fill in."

Jerrod nodded and gently nudged Peter. Then he stood, got Peter in his arms, head on his shoulder, and they left the restaurant. Jerrod got Peter into his truck, and Chase followed him. He soon found a parking space just down the street from Jerrod's house. By the time he got out, Jerrod had unlocked the door and was returning to carry Peter inside. Jerrod went right upstairs, and Chase closed and locked the door, then made another check of the basement before sitting on the sofa to wait.

When Jerrod came downstairs, he sat next to him. "So what's happening?"

"First, let me ask something. In the week or so before the fire at your house, did you have anyone in? A workman or anything?"

Jerrod shook his head. "I did most of the repairs that were needed myself, so I didn't have any reason to call someone."

"How about someone who came to you?" Chase prompted, but he didn't want to lead Jerrod too far.

"You mean like the gas company? There was a leak, and they wanted to check out the rest of the house. That was the day before the fire. At first I thought that might have been the cause of the fire."

"No. There was no gas leak." He waited for the information to sink in.

Jerrod gasped. "I never put it together. It was the day before, and I guess I completely forgot about it. You really think that was how they got inside?"

"It's possible, considering there have been at least three other fires with a similar pattern. Tonight we found and disarmed a device in Red's basement that would have started a fire. When that happened, I wanted to make sure you and Peter were safe. That's all that mattered. I've checked the basement here twice, and there is nothing down there. But whoever is behind this is getting bolder. They even went after a police officer. So whoever is doing this is not afraid of anything, including the police. But there is a silver lining. The last person they tried to burn out had a doorbell camera, and it might have caught them on video. The police are going through that now." He took Jerrod's hand. "I know it may not seem like it, but we are getting closer."

"I know you are. But I could have sworn that I smelled gas in the house," Jerrod said softly.

Chase groaned. He hated bursting his bubble, but he truly thought the gas people were real. "Damn," Chase said softly.

Jerrod jumped slightly. "My phone." He pulled it out and paled before showing Chase the text message. "Gizelle."

I know Peter is in danger because of you. After your house, what else will have to happen before they realize that Peter is safer with me?

"Jesus," Chase said. "Be sure to keep that message, and we'll send it to Red in the morning." He sat back. "Look, I'm not a lawyer, but I looked at stuff online. They aren't going to retry the case like she thinks. All she can do is appeal, and they will look at any irregularities. If the law was followed, they are not going to reopen anything. Her rights will remain terminated. And this behavior isn't going to help her anyway."

"I know. But she…. All this…." He leaned against Chase, and Chase held him tightly.

"Try to take it one day at a time. We've made sure the house is safe, and we aren't going to let anyone we don't know inside. If someone does show up claiming to be from the gas company, just ask them to wait and call the police. Let them sort it out." Chase was getting edgy as well. Someone really seemed to have their finger on what was going on in town and who was doing what as far as construction was concerned. "I have to ask, who would benefit from all this?"

"Any of the other big construction firms. They all wanted the job. It's a great development, and it's supposed to help a number of people. Part of the development will be luxury apartments and condo units, but others will be smaller and much more affordable. In the end, there's a lot of money to be made."

"Yeah, okay. But who is big enough to take on a job like this?" Chase asked.

"Well, a job this size would draw firms from Harrisburg or even Philadelphia. They would come in here and put this up quickly."

Chase nodded, thinking that maybe he was seeing a pattern. "And let me guess—they would bring in their own suppliers, and it would be hard for the borough or anyone associated with it to keep a good watch on them. They could cut corners and put up these expensive units with cheaper materials and make even more."

"Yeah. There are standards in the building codes, but the borough set specific ones for this redevelopment, and I bet they would make things look like they were living up to them. But if the AR backs out, they'd sweep in like a rescuer to 'save' the project, look good, and get the job done without too many questions, because the last thing the borough wants is a project site sitting unfinished. That would not look good at all."

"I don't suppose it would. But why would the borough lower their standards for a new contractor?" Chase asked.

"They wouldn't necessarily, but they would be grateful enough to whoever steps in that things might get overlooked and it wouldn't matter too much because it isn't like there could be a third contractor. So they could accept lower quality, or the project goes dormant and everyone loses, especially the people who have their money in this project."

"You know a lot about this stuff," Chase said softly.

"After working with the people in borough hall, you get to know them. They're good people who really work for the residents and property owners, but with a project this size… let's just say that a contractor who cuts corners and gets away with it could make a lot of money on this job."

"Okay. So who would that be?" Chase asked. "You have to know the people in this area. Who would do that sort of thing?"

"I don't really know. Everyone in the surrounding area is known to everyone else. The market isn't that big. and if anyone were cutting corners, we would all know." He sat back, thinking. "But I will say that a contractor who cuts corners might hire a pair of electricians who would do the same thing. Maybe we should try to talk to the guys I had to let go. They could be a valuable source of information."

Chase nodded. That seemed like a pretty good idea. "Do you think they'll talk to you?"

"Not a chance in hell," Jerrod said. "But I do know one person that at least one of them will speak to, if for no other reason than to get his butt out of trouble for trying to scam me as well as her. Rosemary West is one person no one wants to get on the bad side of, especially in this town. She runs the electrical supply, and unless you want to get everything from Home Depot and deal with them, you have to go to her, especially for anything out of the ordinary." He actually sounded gleeful.

"So what do you think we should do?" Chase asked.

"In the morning, I'll give Rosemary a call and ask her to arrange a meeting with our wayward electrician so they can discuss how he is going to make his account whole, and when he comes in, you and I will be waiting to have a little discussion with him. It could turn out be quite interesting." He sighed and yawned. "I don't know about you, but this has been exhausting, and I think we need to go up to bed." Jerrod stood and took Chase by the hand, leading him up the stairs and down to his room before closing the door behind them.

CHAPTER 14

JERROD HUNG up the phone with a smile and went to call Chase right away. He paused a moment to think about how important Chase had become to him and Peter in such a short period of time and the change that seemed to have come over him. He never would have imagined a few weeks ago that whenever something happened in his life, he would have someone to pick up the phone and share it with. Now he didn't even think about it; he just called Chase. What was more, he knew Chase would be there, which was almost a strange sensation that he still had to completely process.

"I'll be off shift in half an hour," Chase said once Jerrod explained what was happening. "I should be able to meet you there." Just as they were about to end the call, an alarm went off behind him and Chase said he had to go but would message him. Then the line went silent and the call dropped.

And just like that, a new sensation washed over Jerrod: worry. He knew that Chase was most likely out on a call, and he hoped he would be safe.

The very reason that Chase was even in their lives was because of his job and the way he had rescued Peter. Yet at this moment, Jerrod found himself wishing that Chase had a different, safer job. Of course it was stupid—being a firefighter was part of who Chase was—but as he became more and more important to Jerrod, Jerrod wanted him around, and he was well aware that the very job that had brought Chase into his life in the first place could be the thing that did the exact opposite.

"Daddy, is something wrong?" Peter asked.

Jerrod shook his head, forcing the thoughts from his mind. "No. Mr. Chase is out on a call, helping someone." He made himself smile before scooping Peter up into his arms. "Let's get going. I'm taking you to day care and then I need to see Miss Rosemary."

Peter's eyes widened. "The lady with the candy on her desk?" Of course that was what he remembered. Rosemary always had a large bowl on the corner of her desk, and it was filled with chocolates and more. Rosemary herself was diabetic and never touched the stuff unless her sugar dropped too low.

He decided to ignore that or else he'd have Peter begging to go with him. "Go get your shoes on and we'll get going." He watched Peter scramble upstairs. While he waited for him to come back down, Jerrod took a call from the insurance adjustor. His chest tightened when he saw the number.

"I wanted to let you know that everything has been cleared. The final numbers are being run. I'd like to make an appointment for next week so we can go over everything so you know what to expect and the process you'll need to follow going forward. We got your household inventory information, and that has been approved as well. An initial check will be sent based on current valuation. As items are replaced, keep your receipts so any differences can be paid to you."

Jerrod sighed softly. "Thank you. That's very helpful. But what about the house itself?"

"The building will be demolished at this point. The foundation of the house was solid enough but would not stand up to current building code, so if you wish, you can rebuild on the site, but it will have to be a complete rebuild. You should think about your next steps. If you wish to rebuild, then we can help with that process. If you wish to purchase a new home, we can aid with that as well. Take a little time and decide what you want to do." Suddenly, once again, it felt like he had to make huge decisions rather quickly. "There is no clock on those decisions. If you have questions, we can talk them over when we meet next week."

"Thank you." Jerrod forced his stomach to unclench. This was going to be okay. It was just a step in the process, and maybe it would be best if he simply bought a new home and moved on from there. "I appreciate all your help." They agreed on a date and time to meet and then ended the call.

Jerrod took a few seconds to stop his thoughts from running in circles. There were decisions to be made, but he had time. Nothing had to be done now. He kept telling himself all that until Peter came back down the stairs.

"I'm ready to see the candy lady," Peter said with a grin.

Jerrod snatched him into his arms and flew him through the air. "Oh you are, huh?" Peter giggled, and Jerrod blew a raspberry on his belly before setting him on his feet. "I have to take you day care, but I'll take you to see Miss Rosemary soon." He took Peter's hand, and they left the house and got into the truck. He buckled Peter into his car seat before heading out to the day care, where Peter was very good about joining his friends. Then, once he was settled, Jerrod headed to West Electric.

His good mood lasted until he saw smoke just to the north of where they drove on High Street heading to the east. He tried to think of what might be in that direction and sent a silent thought out into the universe that Chase would be safe and that this wasn't another suspicious fire. The last thing he wanted was for anyone else to go through what he had been these past few weeks.

For a second, he thought about heading that way to check on Chase, but of course he'd just be in the way. Instead, he continued out until he reached the light tan pole building that housed West Electric, then pulled around the back and parked next to Rosemary's Audi. He took a second to gather his thoughts before getting out of the truck.

"Come on in," Rosemary said from the back door, then led them inside and down to her office. "Mr. Wilson is going to be here in half an hour," she said as she closed her door. Jerrod sat in one of the office chairs. "Now, can you tell me what you think is going on?"

"There have been a lot of fires in town, and a number of them seem to be linked. One of them is the large fire that burned the supplies at the new condo construction site a few days ago. What we think is that there is someone who is trying to burn out the competition."

"We?" Rosemary asked. "Is there a mouse in your pocket?"

"It's quite a story, and one I'll tell you when we have more time. But Chase—he's a firefighter—first recognized the issue. I'm trying to help him track this down. He knows fire, I know the construction industry in the area…. Anyway, I know it's a bit of a long shot, but someone is putting the squeeze on in order to force the current contractor out of the project. I know it, but I don't know who is behind it."

She nodded, her shoulder-length hair waving slightly as she moved. Rosemary was a knockout, with intense eyes that stopped just about everyone in their tracks. She was also smart as hell and nobody's fool. "And you think Steve Wilson does?"

This was the leap of faith. "I think he might. This is a bit of a stretch. But the more I learn about him, the more I think he's just bright enough to get sucked into something like that. There is no way he'd talk to me."

"I see. And you think if he does know anything that he'd spill his guts to me?"

Jerrod nodded. "I think you have leverage with him because of the bill that's coming due. And even if he isn't involved, a little pressure might get him to tell what he knows. Steve knows things without a doubt. He's too plugged in to what's going on not to. It's how a guy like that survives."

She seemed to ponder what he was saying. "Okay. There is only so much I can do. But the guy did try to cheat both of us, so I'm not opposed to leaning on him to see what we can get out of him. But I draw the line at any sort of deal regarding his bill. He will pay every penny or so help me I will roast his… butt… on a spit." Her eyes darkened, and Jerrod had no doubt she meant it.

"Thank you." He checked his phone for a message. Jerrod wished that Chase was here with him, but if he went out on that last call, then there was no telling how long he would be. Still, with Rosemary's help, they might be able to get some information.

"All right. I'll put the pressure on him to see if I can rattle him and get him off guard. You can add more pressure because he put the charges on your account, and then we'll exact our price and see what information he can give us." Rosemary definitely had a killer instinct. "I don't know if he can tell us anything, but I get the feeling that something is happening and no one is really talking about it."

Jerrod leaned forward slightly. "How do you know?"

"I don't. It's just a feeling… and I don't like it."

A knock sounded on the door, and then Kurt poked his head in. "Steve is here."

"Okay."

While he waited for Steve to come in, Jerrod sent a message to Chase, but he hadn't received a reply by the time Steve came in. His eyes widened in surprise when he saw Jerrod. "What's he doing here?"

Rosemary hit him with an icy glare. "Since it's possible that you tried to steal from him as well as me, I thought he should take part in our conversation." She leaned back as Steve shifted his weight from foot to foot.

"We've been through all of Jerrod's invoices for the past few months, and we've discovered a number of discrepancies… and they all lead back to you."

"That was an innocent mistake. I thought that the charges were going on my account," Steve said.

Rosemary snorted. "I pulled all your invoices, and since very little was charged on your account during that period, I'd say either that's total bullshit, or that's what you have between your ears. Do you want to try that again?" Damn, she was good. "All the charges you made have been transferred to your account, which is due and payable immediately." She handed him a thick stack of papers. "As in right the hell now."

Steve paled and began to wobble as Jerrod stood next to Rosemary. "I sure hope you have the money. We have paperwork and witnesses that you specifically had your items charged to my account under false pretenses," Jerrod said. "So what are you going to do about it?" Maybe if he shook the leaves off the trees, he might come up with something good.

"I can get the money, but I'm going to need a few days. I have some really lucrative jobs on the horizon that will take care of this." Sweat broke out on Steve's brow, and Jerrod knew he was lying through his teeth.

"And what sort of jobs are those?" Rosemary asked. "They wouldn't have anything to do with the development on the north side of town, would they?" She gave him a glare, and Jerrod knew that they did.

"You do realize that I'm the electrical contractor on that job." He watched Steve very closely.

"Only if the general contractor doesn't change." The slight curl of his lip made Jerrod want to smack him. His phone vibrated in his pocket, and he pulled it out to glance at the message from Chase that he was on his way over.

"And why would that happen?" He shoved the phone back in his pocket. "The fire department is aware that the fire was set intentionally, and the police are well into their investigation. Do you think for one second that they aren't going to scour the records and dealings of anyone who tries to push them out and step in?" Now it was his turn to smile as he drew even closer. "Maybe I should take out my anger and frustration at being burned out of my home by the same assholes who set fire to the construction site on you." He let his smile fade and his eyes harden. "I'm sure Rosemary isn't going to see a damned thing if I decide to beat the living shit out of you right here and now."

"What the fuck?" Steve asked. Fear filled his eyes as his composure broke. "I had nothing to do with any of this. I was just offered the electrical contract if they took over." Now they might be getting somewhere.

"Who are *they*?" Jerrod demanded.

Steve shook his head, fear increasing to the point Jerrod could almost smell it.

"If those people are behind this and you are in bed with them, then if any of these fires are linked to them, you will be implicated." He didn't know that for sure, but he figured Steve definitely didn't. "They burned down my house, and they did the same thing to the guy who was supposed to install the AC units. Left his family homeless in the night, watching their house burn. Mine has been destroyed, along with almost everything in it." He gritted his teeth. "Peter could have been killed." He was going to pile it on, forgetting that Rosemary was there. "You'd better fucking tell me what I want to know."

Steve shivered. "I don't know anything."

"Other than who wants to replace AR so badly they'll even make promises to others in case it comes to pass."

Steve turned to Rosemary, who gave him no quarter. "Don't look at me. I'm not going to come to your aid. The only thing I'm going to do is call your account and, if you don't pay, take you to court as well as turn you in to the union and have your license suspended. I'll let Jerrod here tear your cowardly ass apart right here in my office and not see a thing."

"If I tell you they might burn me out too," Steve said softly. "I have a family as well."

"Let me put it this way: if you don't tell us, then we'll call the police right now and you can explain to them exactly what you know and what you don't. I'm sure they'll be more than interested in that, as well as how you used someone else's account." Man, she had brass balls and wasn't afraid to use them.

"Okay." He put his hands up. "It was Connor Warfield. They put in a bid for the job, but it wasn't accepted, but they said that the owners were reconsidering."

"My ass," Rosemary said softly. "They should never be allowed to do business anywhere. Those people are the worst kind of crooked. But I thought they stayed closer to Philly, where they're protected. It looks like they're trying to branch out." Rosemary picked up the phone and made a call while Jerrod called Chase, intending to leave a message.

"I'm just pulling in," he said with an almost forced calm. "I have news."

"Me too. We have the name of the firm. Connor Warfield. But I'm not sure what we should be doing with the information. We can call Red and let him look into it."

"Definitely. I'll be right there." He hung up, and Jerrod wondered what was going on.

Rosemary ended her call with a smile. "The codes officer at the borough was very keen to hear what I had to tell him. He'll be in touch with the owners so they can take action on who might have tried to send them a message. And I think a friend of mine at one of the television stations might be interested in this latest development as well."

Steve sank into one of the chairs, clearly shaken. "What the hell am I going to do?"

"Nothing. You say nothing to anyone. Keep your damned mouth shut. This meeting was about a bill dispute and nothing more. You have the perfect cover for being here. Now I suggest you go out front and make a purchase and a show of carrying it out to your truck before going home." Jerrod didn't like the guy, but he didn't want him to get hurt. "Act normal and no one is going to be the wiser."

Rosemary was on the phone again. "Yeah, you can treat this as a tip." She continued to explain what they had learned. "Just report that a firm from Philadelphia with possible underworld connections seems to be trying to muscle into the area. That's all you need to do and these worms will crawl back into their own hole and leave us alone. They like the darkness and shadow. Yeah. … Good. Yes, this is related to the fire and possibly others in this area." She ended the call and sat down at her desk.

"You sold me out," Steve said with more than a little panic in his voice.

"Hardly. Just do as we told you and go about your business. No one needs to know what you said here or that your coming in here was anything other than business." She motioned toward the door. Steve turned to Jerrod like he was supposed to help him. "You made your bed with your own behavior. Don't expect Jerrod or anyone else to come to your rescue. Your only chance is to keep your mouth shut, settle your bills, and get your business on the straight and narrow, otherwise you aren't going to have one for much longer."

Jerrod had to love Rosemary. Steve looked at each of them once more and then huffed before stomping out of the office.

Jerrod closed the door. "Thanks for that."

"Hey, good people are worth supporting," she said. "Now, I need to get back to work. I'll let you know if anything comes of our tip, but if I know my friend, he's already digging into the story. If there is anything to it that he can prove, then they'll run with it and whatever is going on here with be out in the open. Connor Warfield Construction will find themselves in a bunch of hot water, and their pressure tactics are going to melt away faster than snow in July."

A knock sounded and Chase poked his head inside. "Sorry to bother you, but they said Jerrod was in here."

"We're about done," Rosemary said.

Jerrod thanked her again, then joined Chase out in the hallway. "I've got lots to tell you."

Chase nodded, his expression bleak. "So do I, and I think what I have to tell you is best done at your place." He turned, and they both left. He got into the truck and followed Chase home and inside, where he closed the door. "Look, the investigation is still going on and we're trying to piece together the details of exactly what happened. But you might be aware that in the back of Seven Gables Park, those woods have been a hangout for various unhoused families. At times there have been as many as twenty tents and other shelters out there. The police have been hesitant to clear out the area because the folks don't have another place to go and they would only scatter and try to find other places." Chase sat down, and Jerrod did the same, knowing that Chase was getting around to something.

"Okay. I think I saw something about that on one of the local news boards."

"Yeah, well. It's been a windy day, and that area has quite a bit of underbrush. It seems a fire got started, probably by someone cooking on an open flame, but we're still figuring out the case. Because of the wind, it blew through the shelters and tents, burning everything in a matter of minutes. Three people are dead, and a number have been taken to the hospital." Chase paused, and Jerrod found himself leaning forward, wondering what he was getting at.

"I'm sorry." He figured that any fire scene where people died had to get to Chase. "I know stuff like that has to be hard, and I've always wondered how you dealt with it." He took Chase's hand, not wanting him to feel alone. "What can I do to help?"

CHAPTER 15

CHASE HAD hoped that this would be easier, but Jerrod seemed to have no idea what he was getting at. It warmed his heart that Jerrod's first thought was for him, but Chase's worries were much closer to home—for Jerrod. "It's always difficult because you wonder if you could have saved them if you had been just a few seconds faster. But that isn't the point, at least not in this case." He swallowed and drew closer to Jerrod. "One of the bodies we found had Gizelle's identification in what was left of the belongings. The body was pretty badly burned, and the coroner will need to work on a positive identification, but I think we need to go on the assumption that Peter's mother is dead." He had no idea how Jerrod would take the news.

"God," he whispered softly and then sighed. "I don't know what I should feel. Part of me is relieved that if it's her, then all the issues with her appeals regarding Peter are over, but part of me is sad for him that he will never really know his mother. I had always hoped that she might get herself together and that if nothing else, Peter might be able to get to know her, at least on some level. But now…." He lowered his head and sighed deeply once more. "I know that was a pie-in-the-sky hope. It was never likely that Gizelle would be able to change. And I know she could never have been trusted to care for Peter, but maybe someday they could have had a relationship of some kind…."

Chase squeezed Jerrod's hand. "Is that what you really feel or what you're saying because you think you should?"

Jerrod sat back for a second, his gaze locking on Chase's. "What I am is relieved beyond all hell. She isn't going to be showing up at the door at all hours, trying to insinuate herself into our lives. And Peter will never have to deal with her chaos. That was always the price with Gizelle. She had her good moments, but they were always wrapped in this chaotic energy that seemed to never end. Peter doesn't need that, and thankfully we won't have to deal with that any longer." He looked up. "Does that make me a bad person?"

"No. It makes you honest. Gizelle was a threat to your family, and now that's gone. I think I'd be relieved too if I were in your shoes. But I also think that it's a shame Peter will never know his mother." It was a double-edged issue. Chase wished he had an answer for Jerrod. "Whatever you feel, it isn't my place to judge you or to tell you what you should do from here. You and your brother were the ones who had to deal with her and had to look out for Peter." Chase checked the time. "Speaking of him, don't you need to pick him up?"

"Yeah." Jerrod got to his feet, his shoulders seeming weighed down.

"I can wait here if you like. Otherwise I can head home, and you can decide what you want to say to Peter, if anything, on your own. It's up to you." Chase wasn't sure what Jerrod would want.

Jerrod seemed lost for a moment. "Thanks. Umm, stay, please."

Chase nodded, and Jerrod grabbed his keys and hurried out. Chase sat back, pulled out his phone, and found an app to help pass the time.

CANDY CRUSH was a great time waster, and soon enough, a key shook in the lock. Peter rushed in with papers clutched in his hand, fluttering in the breeze he created. "I made something for you." He pushed the papers at Chase, who took each drawing.

"These are wonderful."

"That's a horse." He pointed to one drawing. "And this one is you and Daddy on a horse, and this one is me on a pony. I also drew Papa on a horse, but I had to imagine what he looked like, since he is in heaven."

Chase smiled at the man with wings on a brown horse shape. It was imaginative and clever. "I like the wings." Chase loved the smile Peter flashed at him. He was clearly pretty proud of them.

Peter nodded. "Daddy says Papa is an angel now and that he's watching over me to keep me safe." He hurried away just as quickly as he came up, running up the stairs.

"I couldn't tell him. Apparently, they talked about families in day care, so Peter got to thinking about Johnny and started drawing pictures. I don't know where the horses came from, but it's something that he seems fascinated with at the moment."

Chase checked out the drawings again. "There's no time frame. You could wait to tell him until we hear from the coroner that it's definitely her. There's no need to put him through anything until it's official."

"How long will that take?"

"I understand that dental records have already been ordered, and since she was local, it shouldn't take too much time before they are able to check them. These sorts of things take a day or two. I know it sucks, and maybe I shouldn't have said anything, but I wanted you to know what was going on." There had been so much uncertainty in their lives already, and Chase hated to add to it.

"That's what we'll do. Let's be sure, and then we can tell him."

Chase smiled at the fact that Jerrod used *we*. He liked being part of a *we*, even if it was for something as unpleasant as this.

"That is probably best. He doesn't seem to remember her much." He had seen her and had no real connection, though Gizelle was acting a little crazy at the time.

"No. Johnny was always the parent in the family. I'm sure Peter has specific memories of her from when he was smaller, but Gizelle hasn't been part of his life since he was two and a half. He does remember Johnny."

"I see that."

"Yeah. I was going to tell him about Gizelle, and instead he asked about his papa, so I told him a few stories. He said that he had been thinking about Papa a lot because he was in heaven and that he was almost there too until he was saved by Mr. Chase." Jerrod shook his head slowly. "Sometimes he scares me at just how much he knows and how he puts things together. Someday that kid is either going to solve climate change or try to take over the world. Who knows?"

"Yeah, I get it." Chase took Jerrod in his arms and hugged him closely. "All we can do is take things one step at a time." He closed his eyes, letting Jerrod's earthy scent surround him. "You told me that you had some news too." Maybe it was a good time to change the subject, though he had no intention of letting Jerrod go.

"Yeah. I found out who might be behind the fires. A construction company out of Philly is trying to muscle in. It's pretty complicated, but it seems someone at Connor Warfield is trying to push AR out. They apparently submitted a bid, but it was rejected. Word is that they use inferior materials and cut corners. But with some muscle…."

"AR decides they can't stand the heat and backs out. Connor Warfield steps in, brings in their own subcontractors, and the job goes on, only with shoddy work that everyone pays for for years."

"Exactly. Rosemary put a bug in a reporter friend's ear, so it's likely all this is going to come out in a few days. The best thing you can do is alert the department so they can have details of their investigation ready. There are going to be lots of questions, and people are going to want answers."

"Yeah, they are." Chase needed to call Hayden to give him a heads-up. They were aware that the fires were linked, but not about the connections. Still, he didn't want to move away. It was great just being here with Jerrod. He closed his eyes, letting contentment wash over him.

"Daddy, I want hugs too," Peter said, racing over. Jerrod lifted him and then hugged Chase as well, the three of them standing quietly until Peter squirmed and declared that he was hungry.

JERROD CAME back down the stairs after putting Peter to bed. "Is he asleep?"

"I hope so. He asked me to tell him stories of Papa, and once I finished one, he wanted another." Jerrod sat down. "I suppose I should have expected it."

Chase leaned back. "That's why he left Peter with you. Your brother knew you would be the one to tell Peter all about him. So it's good that you're sharing things."

"Yeah. I told Peter about the time we visited the farm of a friend of our mother's. I ran up to one of the fences, and there was a cow on the other side, staring back at me. Apparently, she was an ornery cow tried to charge the fence. Johnny pulled me back and began yelling at the cow, and she ambled off. Johnny then took me to see the goats. I liked the goats and got to pet them and stuff. Then we saw the chickens, which were no fun at all. Peter asked me if he could get a goat."

"What did you tell him?"

"That the borough doesn't allow goats in town. I figured that was a good answer. Then Peter said that since he couldn't have a goat, did the borough allow dogs? What was I supposed to tell him then?"

Chase shrugged. "You could get him a dog. It would be good for him."

Jerrod rolled his eyes. "But I don't like dogs. My mother had a little poodle growing up, and that thing hated me. My parents got the dog because they thought it would be a great pet for Johnny and me. Instead he loved Mom and had little to do with the rest of us." He groaned.

"Then get a different kind of dog. Maybe take Peter to the dog rescue outside of town and let him pick one out himself."

"But I work and Peter will go to school. It isn't fair to leave a dog home alone all the time."

"Then get Peter a cat. He'll love it, and they are much more self-sufficient. But if he's asking for a pet, he probably isn't going to stop." Chase sat next to Jerrod. "You don't need to get him one today or tomorrow. Maybe make it a reward for him." He squeezed Jerrod's hand. "What do you think your brother would do?"

"He'd get Peter the damned dog," Jerrod said softly. "He always wanted a pet of his own, but Mom would never let us get another. So yeah, he'd get Peter the dog." He sat down and groaned. "Okay, I can do that. Anything for Peter and Johnny."

"Jerrod, it's only a dog, and getting one will make Peter happy. I love dogs, and when the time comes, I can help you pick out a good one that will fit for you and for Peter. Now, do you want to talk about something else?"

Jerrod swallowed hard and nodded slowly. "Like what?"

"I don't know. We could talk about the weather in Amsterdam in July or about the latest in wedding fashion, but…."

Jerrod rolled his eyes and slipped his hand around the back of Chase's neck, pulling him in for a kiss that turned almost brutal in seconds, not that Chase was complaining.

"Is that what you want?" Chase whispered. "You want it hard?"

Jerrod groaned and kissed him harder, sending a wave of molten heat through Chase. "Yeah."

"Then lead the way."

Chase followed that amazing ass up the stairs and down to the bedroom. Chase closed the door before grabbing Jerrod in his arms and tossing him on the bed. "You asked for rough." He expected Jerrod to back off, but he pulled Chase down by the scruff of his shirt and kissed him with an intensity of passion that Chase had never known. Well, if Jerrod wanted intense and hard, that was what he was going to get. He pulled Jerrod's shirt off before getting his own over his head. "You have about ten seconds to get those clothes off or I'm going to rip those jeans to shreds."

Jerrod was naked in five, and Chase followed, prowling onto the bed, watching Jerrod's huge eyes. He didn't want to overdo it, but it seemed this was what Jerrod needed, and Chase was more than willing to give it to him.

"Chase," Jerrod whispered, his voice rough and deep.

Chase growled softly before taking charge of his lips, determined to transport Jerrod away from the worry and tension that seemed to have him wound tighter than a drum. "I know what you need," Chase whispered and held Jerrod close. "I know this has been hard, and it's been one thing after another."

Jerrod shook his head. "I don't want to talk about fires, insurance, or crazy sisters-in-law. What I want is for you to fuck me into next week. I don't want to be able to think straight after that."

"Oh, baby, I fully intend to." Chase scooted between Jerrod's legs, pushing his knees upward before leaning over him. "You will forget your name by the time I'm through with you, and that's a fucking promise." He pulled Jerrod toward him and kissed hard as he met Jerrod's swirling gaze. "And I always keep my promises. The only thing is that you cannot wake Peter. So you have to be quiet no matter what." He kept his voice low, speaking softly into Jerrod's ear. "No matter how much you want to cry out or tell me to fuck you harder, you have to make as little sound as possible, because if Peter wakes up, I'm going to have to stop."

"Fuck," Jerrod breathed.

"Exactly. I will have to stop the fucking, and that is going to be a real shame." Jerrod's eyes goggled and his breathing became more rapid… and he hadn't really done anything yet.

DAMN, JERROD was hot, covered in sweat, his eyes wide, mouth open, chest heaving, staring up at the ceiling. "Wow."

"That good?" Chase asked, more than a little pleased with himself. Jerrod had nearly lost control, and Chase had had to back away more than once for fear that Jerrod would wake Peter and bring their fun to a close.

"Where in the hell did you learn to do that?" Jerrod whispered. "Never mind, you don't have to tell me. In fact, I don't think I want to know."

Chase scoffed. "Please. It isn't like I worked in a brothel in Bangkok. I'm just naturally gifted." He chuckled when Jerrod did and lay on the now sweat-dampened sheets.

"Can I ask something?"

"Sure," Chase answered, tensing.

"Where is this going?" Jerrod rolled onto his side. "I mean, we seem to get along, and you always seem to be there for us." He sniffed slightly. "I'm not used to having someone there like that, and I think I could really get used to it. But if this is a more casual thing for you, then I need to know. I can't have people waltzing in and out of Peter's life, and to tell you the truth, that isn't what I want either."

Chase gently stroked Jerrod's cheek. "I'm not a casual kind of guy, not anymore. Not with you. At least I don't think so. As for where things are going, I don't know. I've been trying to take my cues from you as much as I can. There has been so much happening that I don't want to put pressure on you. Besides, we don't need to make life-changing decisions today or tomorrow."

"O-kay."

"Jerrod, don't read too much into this. I'm just saying that I don't intend to go anywhere. I like having you and Peter in my life. Being a part of a family is something I've wanted for a long time."

"So I should be patient?"

Chase didn't understand the edge in Jerrod's voice. "Just take things at a pace that's comfortable." He gathered Jerrod to him, and he rested his head on Chase's shoulder. "Like you said, this is more than just about you and me, and there is no prescribed timetable. This isn't a book or a movie. This is our romance, and we get to conduct it the way we want."

"Is that what this is? A romance?"

Chase chuckled. "Sure." He drew Jerrod into a kiss. "And if you wait a little while, I can do my best to romance you again, but you gotta give a guy a chance to catch his breath." They shared a smile, and then Chase closed his eyes.

"What is it about these moments? When we're quiet together and it's just the two of us?" Jerrod asked. "They seem.... I don't know."

"Intimate," Chase supplied. "Like it's just you and me and the rest of the world doesn't seem to matter."

"Yeah," Jerrod said softly, tilting his head so they could see each other's eyes. "Maybe it's kind of stupid."

"Caring about someone isn't stupid, and just taking a little time to be together without having to get it on is what a relationship is all about." He smiled. "My parents had this weird way of being together. They were both always so busy. My dad worked his main job, and then he also took a second one part-time to earn extra money. Mom was working too, and they sometimes never saw each other except at night. I had the bedroom next to theirs, and while I could never hear what they were saying, I always knew they were talking. I also know that Mom and Dad had an active sex life."

"And how is that?" Jerrod asked with a snicker.

"Oh God, no, I did not spy on them. But after I was born, Mom got pregnant a number of times but kept losing the baby. Eventually they had my younger sister, Violet, and Mom tried a few more times to have another baby before giving up. Still, they talked every night. It was when they were quiet...." Chase sighed. "Anyway, they always talked and spent the time together in bed."

"Yeah. I read a book a few years ago, and one of the characters said that he always wanted 'someone to do nothing with in bed.' Like it was important and meant more than the fucking."

Chase rolled his eyes. "Sex is important, but so is just being together. Strangers have sex all the time. You just have go into the bathroom of a gay club to see that, usually purposely on display. But how many one-night stands involve talking or cuddling once the sex is over? Usually it's how quickly can I sneak out of here without looking like a weirdo. Hell, half the time, the prince you thought you brought home turns into a frog... fast." They chuckled together, and Jerrod stiffened. "What is it?"

Jerrod got out of bed and opened the closet door, then pulled on a robe. "Just a minute." He opened the door and closed it behind him again. Chase sighed and pulled up the covers, lying quietly for a while until Jerrod returned. "Peter was awake, and I found him crying in bed." He took off the robe and slipped under the covers. "He had a bad dream."

"About the fire?" Chase asked, and Jerrod nodded. "You know, if it will help, I can check to see if the department has someone who works with children to give Peter someone to talk to, help him work through what happened."

"Thanks. He's had a few since you rescued him, and I was hoping they would fade away on their own. But maybe he needs more."

"I'll check and let you know." Chase rolled over, putting his arms around Jerrod.

"Thanks," Jerrod said wearily, and Chase closed his eyes. He wished that Jerrod's headaches were over, but he suspected something else was just around the corner. Chase just wished he could see what it was.

CHAPTER 16

THE LAST two days had been quiet, and Jerrod began to hope that his life was returning to normal.

"Did you see what's happening?" Mr. Dunston asked as he brought Jerrod a cup of coffee. Jerrod was just finishing up the wiring to add a charging port in his garage for his new electric car.

"I haven't been on the internet today. Why?" He sipped and set the mug away from where he was working, then checked that everything was hooked up properly before turning on the power so he could test it.

"You don't think stuff like that could happen in a town like this," he said. "Some firm was trying to muscle their way into town. Penn News just sent me an alert about a story."

"The new condo complex?" Jerrod asked, and Mr. Dunston smiled as he nodded.

"I'm supposed to do the wiring for the units once they're built." He hoped that was still a good contract. He would need the work if he wanted to build the business so he could spend more time with Peter. "What did they say?"

"That the fire on the site was set by this rival firm and that it was possible that other fires in town were linked to them. The state police are involved, as are locals and maybe even the FBI. I don't think I'd want to be these people. Some firm out of Philly, but now they're being looked at there as well. Seems they aren't on the up-and-up." He grinned. "And all because they tried to get away with shit here."

"Yeah, well…." Jerrod returned his attention to the job at hand. "I think one of those fires was mine."

"Holy shit, man. You think so? That's messed up. I hope they nail those bastards to the wall. Is there anything Jean or I can do? You need any help?" He drew closer. "Is the insurance company treating you right? You call me if they aren't." Mr. Dunston was a partner in one of the big law firms in town. "Hell, you call me in the office on Monday and we'll make sure they are. Free of charge. You always did really good work for me, and you always came right out. We Carlislians need to stick together."

Jerrod swallowed around the lump in his throat. "I appreciate that. The insurance company had been stalling because they thought I might have set the fire."

"You call me and we'll make sure that they are doing everything they're supposed to. No problem. I have an associate who does nothing but insurance, and he's really good. He almost never goes to court but gets them to pay up like they should every damned time."

Jerrod flipped the breaker on the electrical box and checked that the charger had power. Then they plugged in Mr. Dunston's Rivian. "It's charging properly."

"Excellent. Thanks for coming out on a Friday afternoon. This whole thing is a present for Jean, and I wanted to make sure she had everything she needed."

"Has she seen the car?" Jerrod asked.

Mr. Dunston shook his head. "Today is her birthday. She's been a little down about getting older, and I know she's been looking at these. Blue is her favorite color, so this will be her surprise when she gets home from her classes." His wife taught American studies at Dickinson College.

"It's a great gift." Jerrod finished his coffee and put away his tools.

"I hope she thinks so." Mr. Dunston waited as he packed up and then walked with him out to his truck. "What's the damage?" he asked.

"Well…." He figured he could do this in trade if Mr. D was willing to help with the insurance company bureaucracy, which was headache inducing, but he wouldn't have it. He paid his bill through a cash app right on the spot.

"You have expenses and bills to pay. Helping you is the least I can do." He smiled and headed up to the front door of the large historic stone home. "Now go pick up that son of yours, and you have a great weekend." He went inside, and Jerrod finished putting away his gear before heading over to the Y.

The entire place was in an uproar. All the kids were sitting on the floor of one of the activity rooms with parents crowded around them.

"What happened?"

"Apparently one of the kids is missing," another parent told him. Instantly, he looked around the room, but didn't see Peter. His heart beat fast enough he became light-headed.

"Where's Peter?" he asked one of the counselors as the director came in. Jerrod's phone rang, and he took Chase's call. "Peter's gone. I'm at his summer day camp and he isn't here."

"God," Chase said. "That body we found that we thought was Gizelle's—it wasn't her."

"She has Peter," Jerrod said.

"Okay. I'm on my way. Call the police. I'm going to see if I can get hold of Red. Don't let anyone leave there, and I'll be over as soon as I can get there." He ended the call, and Jerrod called 911 and explained what was going on and reported that Peter had possibly been abducted. By the time he finished answering their questions, he was surrounded by people, including the executive director.

"The police are on their way. Everyone is to stay here until they get here," Jerrod told her. "Do you have cameras outside the building?"

"Yes. They monitor the parking lot."

"I want to see the footage," he told her. "Right now."

"But the police—"

"Time is of the essence." He needed to see if it was Gizelle. "So show me." He followed her down the hall into a small office. She pulled up the footage from the side parking lot closest to where the kids got out. It took about two minutes before he saw Peter and Gizelle heading across the lot and out of sight of the cameras.

"Do you know her?" the director asked as the police entered the room. He leaned closer, surprised at how quickly she moved and managed to corral Peter away from the others. She must have been watching and waiting for her chance. Damn her.

"Yes. Play them the tape. The woman is Peter's mother, Gizelle Giordano. Her parental rights were terminated by the courts, and she's taken Peter." He took out his phone and pulled up a picture of the court order.

Red nodded, asked for a description, and requested an APB. "Do you know where she might have taken him?"

Jerrod shook his head. "How would I know? She showed up in town a few weeks ago. I don't know where she's been living, except out in the woods where the fire was."

Chase joined them and put his arm around Jerrod's waist. "The police will find him, but they need help. Did Gizelle have a car?"

Jerrod tried to remember. "I'm not sure. She would show up at the house, but I never noticed that she drove anything."

"And she walked out of the camera range, as opposed to getting into a car. Is there someplace close she might know? A place that's familiar?" Red asked.

"Maybe. She and my brother used to live out on Mooreland." He gave them the address.

Red called it in and requested a unit to check it out. "Check out the trails to the west as well."

Jerrod felt helpless and collapsed into one of the chairs in the office, his legs giving out. The police asked more questions; people talked on phones and across radios. All of it quickly became a blur. All he could think of was Peter and the fact that he was gone.

"It's going to be okay. The police are going to find him," Chase said from next to him, but it felt like a dream. Jerrod nodded because he felt he had to. "Stay with us," Chase said, kneeling down to meet his gaze. "Take a few deep breaths. The police are out looking for him, and they aren't going to stop. Red is on the phone with the state police just in case she has a car. They are putting out alerts all over the state. She isn't going to be able to move without someone seeing her."

Jerrod groaned. "I just want Peter back and for him to be safe. I should have made sure he was safe. I...."

Chase hugged him. "This isn't your fault. Gizelle tried to fake her own death. I bet she was planning something like this." Jerrod shook in his arms, trying to keep himself together, even as he felt the first cracks begin to spider through him. This was his fault. He should have kept Peter safer. He....

"Just breathe and try to stay calm so you can think. You need to help Peter, and that means staying alert and strong for him."

He nodded, doing as Chase told him, breathing slowly and steadily. "I'm trying."

"Okay. Think about what you know about Gizelle," Chase told him.

"That would be helpful," Red said after listening to the radio. "She isn't at the house on Mooreland. The family there hasn't seen anyone. We're still scouring the area, but there isn't any sign of her. If she did take him, then she would have had to have planned to take him somewhere."

"And it's probably nearby," Chase added.

"I don't know. Peter isn't going to be happy about going with her. He doesn't know her very well."

"Okay," Chase said softly. "If you were on foot and took someone, would you hide out, or go someplace with lots of people so you could get lost?"

"I have people checking out the area around the Walmart and the shopping center. Officers are also at the theater."

"Thornwald Park," Jerrod said. "In the back, near the mansion, there's that old children's theater and the trail back toward the highway. No one goes back there much, and it's a great place to hide out. I remember Gizelle used to love hanging out back there. She and Johnny used to go there to make out before they got married." Maybe there was some hope. But the longer this went on, the more distance she and Peter could cover and the less likely it became that they would be found.

"Good idea," Red said, calling it in. "Be careful and don't make a huge show of presence." He continued talking.

"Maybe we should get you home," Chase said. "Sitting here in the Y isn't helping anyone. The police are doing what they can, and we need to let Red get on out there."

Jerrod nodded and got to his feet. Chase took him by the arm and led him out to the parking lot. They got into Jerrod's truck, and he handed Chase the keys and let him drive home while Jerrod stared at his phone, willing it to ring with news. "I want to go out there and look for them myself."

"I know, but that's a bad idea. We need to let the professionals handle this. We'd only be in the way." Chase parked in front of the house, and Jerrod got out and let them inside. Peter had left some toys on the sofa that morning, and Jerrod gathered them and placed them on the coffee table. He sat and held his head in his hands. Jerrod wanted to cry and shout, but mostly he would give anything to have Peter back with him safe and sound.

"Here's some water," Chase said quietly.

Jerrod took the glass. After a few seconds, he barely knew it was there, his attention all focused on Peter. His phone chimed, and he set the glass aside, ready to answer, but it was only an app notification, and he groaned before setting the phone back on the table.

"How long has it been?" Jerrod asked.

"About two hours," Chase answered.

It seemed like a lifetime. Jerrod's throat threatened to close up, and he leaned back, concentrating on breathing. The waiting was excruciating. He needed to know something.

Finally, fifteen minutes later, his phone rang and he snatched it up. "Yes. This is Jerrod."

"It's Red. We have Peter. He's fine, and I'm going to bring him over to you." Jerrod could barely believe the words. "He wasn't hurt. We'll tell you everything in a few minutes. We expect to be there soon."

Jerrod ended the call, and the phone slipped from his hand and landed on the cushions of the sofa.

"He's fine. Red is bringing him home," he managed to say to Chase, overwhelmed with relief. Still, he sat at the window until the cruiser pulled up out front. Then he hurried outside as Red got Peter out of the car. He knelt down and held open his arms as Peter ran to him.

"I'm okay, Daddy. Mommy took me to the movies," he reported, seemingly none the worse for wear. Jerrod hugged him, tears streaming down his face as he held his son, trying to keep from squeezing him. "It was fun. She took me to see *Puss in Boots*, and it was funny but sad too. I like Perrito a lot. Then Mr. Red said that he was going to bring me home." He jabbered on about the movie and something about a wishing star, but all Jerrod cared about was that Peter was safe at home.

"Can we go inside?" Red asked.

Jerrod took Peter's hand and led them into the house. Peter hurried up to Chase for a hug and then ran up the stairs the way he always did.

"He has no idea," Red said. "We found them in the theater, coming out of the movie. One of the officers explained to Peter that you were waiting for him and called me. I came to get him, and once he was out of her sight, we took Gizelle into custody. We were able to get Peter away before she began screaming and tried to get to him again. We had to restrain her. She'll spend the night in jail and will be charged, but we'll have to have her evaluated. I don't think she's competent to stand trial. She actually thought that she and Peter were on some outing and that taking him was no big deal. She got him popcorn. It was like they were just seeing a movie instead of a kidnapping." He sighed.

"Thank you for finding him. I don't know how I can thank you enough." He knew he had tears tracked down his cheeks, and Chase placed his hand lightly on his back. "Both of you."

"I'm just glad we were able to get him back home and that he doesn't seem upset about all of it. Peter is completely unaware of all the worry that went on, and it's probably best he doesn't know. Let him just think it was his mother taking him to the movies."

"How did you get him in the police car without making a big deal of it?"

Red smiled. "I told him that you had asked me to give him a ride and that we could turn the lights on and everything. He was so excited to ride in a police car that he didn't think anything of it." He lowered his voice. "This way there's no trauma to him, and while you were worried sick, he's still the happy little boy he always was."

Jerrod nodded and realized that they were right. He might be a complete mess, but Peter was fine, and that was what counted. "It's probably the best thing."

Chase walked Red to the door. "Is there anything else we need to do?"

"Not at the moment. Until Gizelle is evaluated, there isn't a lot that we can get out of her. It is going to be a few days, but I hope that I'll be able to speak with her and get some information about what she did and what she was thinking. I do know that she isn't going to be released no matter what. After this, she'll either be tried or placed in a mental hospital to get treatment. This episode demonstrates that she is indeed a danger to others."

"Thank you and the department for everything," Chase said.

"Yeah, thank you so much." Jerrod shook Red's hand before Chase let him out. Once he was gone, Jerrod collapsed in the chair. "I don't think I can ever go through that again. I—"

"Daddy," Peter called, bounding down the stairs. "Where Rexxy?"

"Right here." Jerrod held up the stuffed dinosaur. Peter cuddled the stuffed toy to his chest and then hurried back upstairs to most likely put him where he belonged. Then he came back down and climbed into Jerrod's lap.

"What's wrong, Daddy? Are you sad?" Peter leaned against Jerrod's chest.

Jerrod closed his eyes, just holding his son. "I'm okay now that you're here. I promise."

"I'm good at making people happy, right?" Peter said.

Jerrod smiled lightly. "You are." He took a deep breath as Chase's hand settled on his shoulder. Jerrod placed one hand on top of it and tried to hold on to the fact that he had both of them and that everyone was okay. Peter was home and in his arms. Chase was here as well, and he'd been there the whole time. He was lucky to have that support.

"How about I order Chinese for dinner?" Chase asked.

"I'm hungry," Peter said. "Mommy got popcorn at the movies, but it was floor popcorn, so I didn't want to eat any." Peter slipped down off his lap, running out of the room, and Jerrod shook his head, groaning, and bit his lower lip to keep from saying anything.

"It's okay. He's here and back home safe," Chase said softly and squeezed his shoulder.

"What the hell am I going to do?" What kind of life was this? In the past few weeks, his house had burned down, Peter had been kidnapped, and there was still an arsonist out there. What kind of life could he offer Peter or Chase? Hell, what the fuck was going to happen next? Suddenly Jerrod could barely breathe.

"It's okay. Take deep breaths. This is only a little panic, and you need to relax. In and out, deep and slow," Chase said. "That's it. Close your eyes and just listen to the sound of my voice. Breathe in and out and this is going to pass."

"I wish it would. I really wish all of this would just go away," he whispered.

"That isn't what you really want. It's only how things feel at this moment. I know it's hard and that everything seems to be piling on right now, but you and Peter are okay. He's home and he's safe, so just relax and breathe. That's it."

Jerrod kept his eyes closed as the tightness in his chest eased. He said nothing, doing his best to push away the fear that seemed like black clouds on the edges of his vision. He kept wondering how much more he could take. The world really seemed to be piling the crap on his shoulders lately.

"Better?" Chase asked.

"Yeah, a little," Jerrod said quietly, almost to himself. "How can you be so calm about this?"

"I'm not," Chase said quietly. "I'm worried for you and for Peter, of course I am. When you told me he had been taken, I felt it like a punch in the gut. But I also knew that the best thing I could do was to try to keep my head level so I could help you and Peter." He knelt down. "It's part of what I'm trained to do. Stay calm in a crisis and do my best to work your way out of it. Peter is home, Gizelle is in custody, and she isn't going to be able to pop around here any time she wants to bother you and Peter. Eventually she'll get the help she needs and we can go on with our lives."

"But what if I can't?" Jerrod asked. "I keep thinking that maybe it would be best for Peter and me to leave and start over someplace else. I'll have the money from the house. We could buy a place elsewhere and leave all this behind."

Chase grew quiet. "I see." His hand slipped off Jerrod's shoulder. "Is that what you really want to do?" His voice grew colder and more distant.

Jerrod turned to look at him. "I don't know what the heck I should do. I just want Peter to be safe. That's the most important thing." His head was spinning. "I'm probably just talking off the top of my head, and I'm scared right now, so I'm probably saying dumb things." He held out his hand, and thankfully Chase took it. "I know that if all this hadn't happened—that if I hadn't lost the house and if you hadn't saved Peter—I would never have known you."

"Sometimes things happen for a reason, even bad things."

"That's true. I know that. But it's still a lot to deal with. At this point, Gizelle is out of the picture, and I know that the article appeared about the fires and the construction company, but it doesn't get us any closer to knowing who set fire to my house. Someone did it, and they're still out there. Just because we think they did it at the behest of the Connor Warfield doesn't give us the answers, and we both know they could try again."

"I know that. And I've been thinking about that. But I don't know where to start. Investigations aren't my field of expertise. Maybe we give Red a few days and then see where he is on the arson. He's been a busy guy these past few days."

"Or maybe we see if we can speak with Steve again." Jerrod leaned forward. "I'm sure he knows more than he's telling. The guy is scared out of his wits, and he wasn't going to say anything he thought could get him in any trouble. But I bet once he's had a chance to think, that fear is going to grow, especially after that article in the news."

"Do you know where he lives?"

"Yeah, I do."

"Then next week, after work, let's pay him a visit and shake a few more leaves off the tree and see what falls out." Jerrod nodded. "But for now, let's get you and Peter something to eat and we can watch a movie for a while. Something to take our minds off everything that's happened. Okay?"

Jerrod sighed softly. "Yeah." There was still a threat out there, and they needed to handle it or else Jerrod was never going to feel comfortable in his own home again. But for now, a distraction sounded like a good idea.

CHAPTER 17

CHASE LAY in bed next to Jerrod, worried about him. He hadn't slept and kept getting up in the night. More than once, Chase had found him in Peter's room, sitting in the chair watching him sleep. Finally, Jerrod had dropped off and was now quiet and resting. At least that was what Chase hoped. Chase understood how worried Jerrod had been and that he just needed to see Peter and know that he was okay, but he still worried with everything piling on Jerrod that the weight of it would be too much.

He checked the time and slipped out of bed, grateful it was a Sunday morning. Chase was off shift, and most likely Jerrod didn't have appointments, so he hoped they could have a day to relax and spend some time together. Quietly, he dressed and left the room, finding Peter in his room, playing. "You hungry?" Chase asked.

"Yes." He left what he was playing and followed Chase down the stairs, still in his dinosaur PJs. "Where's Daddy?"

"He's sleeping, and he's really tired," Chase told him.

Peter nodded as though he understood. "He's been grumpy a lot."

"Your daddy has been really worried. He has to deal with the old house and then some other stuff with his work. So what we really need to do is be quiet and let him sleep some more. I was thinking that if you want, I could find some cartoons and you could watch them on my iPad after breakfast."

"Okay." Peter sat down at the table. "Can you make pancakes? I really want those. With blueberries in them."

"I can do that." Chase checked the cupboards until he found some mix and began following the instructions. He also found frozen blueberries and set to work.

"Will Daddy always be sad?" Peter asked.

"No. It's just hard for him right now. But your daddy loves you very much, and I don't think he's going to be sad for very much longer. Maybe what he needs to be not sad is some pancakes. How about we take some to him later?"

"Yeah." Peter seemed excited.

Chase got some small pancakes going in a pan and sprinkled in some blueberries. Once he had a few, he plated them for Peter and helped him butter them. He didn't want syrup, and Chase let him eat as he made himself a stack.

"Are they good?"

"Yummy," Peter said with a grin, shoving more pancake in his mouth.

Chase ate his breakfast before making some fresh pancakes and putting them on a plate. He was looking around for a tray when Jerrod came into the room.

"Daddy, we were going to bring you some."

"Pancakes?" Jerrod asked as Chase set down the plate for him. They shared a smile, and then he dug right in. "These are so good."

"You were tired, Daddy."

"I was. But I'm not now, and maybe after we all get dressed we can go out and have some fun. Would you like that?"

"Yeah. Can we go to the zoo?"

"Lake Tobias?" Chase asked.

"Yay. I like the zoo," Peter declared, and just like that it seemed they had picked their activity for the day. "They have lots of fun animals, and you can even pet some of them." Peter got up and left the room, probably to dress so they could go.

"If you want to spend some time at home, we'll understand," Jerrod said.

"I like the zoo," Chase told him. "But I do need to go home and get some fresh clothes." He cleared the table and put the dishes in the sink. "Maybe you could take me to the Y to get my truck, and then I can run home, change quick, and we can go, if that's okay. I'll understand if you want this to be just you and Peter." He had been spending a lot of time with Jerrod and his tiny family, and maybe they needed some space to themselves.

Peter raced back and slid to a stop. "Mr. Chase, you need to come too," Peter said. "We can see the buck buck buck chickens and the moo moo moo cows." He was so excited.

"Of course I want you to come," Jerrod said. "Give us a few minutes to get dressed and we'll take you over to get your truck." Jerrod lifted Peter into his arms and flew him out of the room. At least some of his tension seemed to have slipped to the background.

As JERROD drove them north of Halifax, Chase and Peter played a game. "What does a peacock say?" Peter asked with giggles. And Chase did his best to imitate their spine-curling cry. Beautiful birds, ugly sound.

"What does an alligator say?" Chase asked in return. Peter thought and then made a roar sound. "Actually, I don't think they make a sound unless it's chomp, chomp." He tickled Peter's belly and got more giggles.

"Daddy, what does a bunny say?" Peter asked.

"I don't know. Do they squeal sometimes?" he asked.

"No. Bunnies are quiet. They eat carrots, so maybe they make noise when they eat. I don't know." That seemed like the definitive answer. "Are we almost there yet?"

"Yes. Just a little longer," Jerrod answered as Chase tried to think of another animal.

"I know. What does a camel sound like?" Chase asked, turning back to Peter, who shrugged. "They make a grunty sound, and if you get them angry, they spit." As the game wound down, they turned into the entrance. Jerrod parked the car, and they climbed out.

"Can we go on the safari?" Peter asked. "I wanna see the giraffes and the lions. Roar...." He bounded away and then came right back, giving them a "what are you waiting for?" look.

"We'll be right there," Jerrod said and then pressed Chase against the side of the truck, kissing him quickly. "Thanks for coming. I think this is going to be fun, and we all deserve some of that."

He smiled, and Chase did the same. Damn, Jerrod could get his motor revved in one hell of a hurry. But this was so not the place for that. Then Jerrod backed away and walked over to take Peter's hand. "Let's go see everything." He had almost as much energy as Peter.

Jerrod paid their admission, and they stepped through the gate, Peter running toward the first enclosure. "Damn." He instantly tensed, his smile fading fast. "That's Steve Wilson with his family." He ground his teeth.

"Okay." In that moment, Chase saw when Steve noticed Jerrod, as a cloud descended over his expression. "Go talk to him a minute. Maybe make sure he's okay after what's come out. I'll take Peter to the lion enclosure, and we'll meet you there." Chase joined Peter, and they headed off to look at the lions, though Chase kept turning back just to make sure Jerrod was okay.

"ISN'T HE pretty?" Peter asked as they stood outside the enclosure. The male lion rested on a rock, sunning himself. "I wish we could get one."

"Lions and big cats like that aren't pets. They're wild animals, and they need to be out in big spaces, hunting and being around other lions."

"Then why is this one in there? Should they take it back?" Peter was such an observant kid, his mind always working.

"You see, he was born in captivity, in a zoo of some sort, and he isn't able to take care of himself in the wild. That's why he's here. But other lions, baby ones, they have a chance to live free." Chase hoped he explained it to Peter in a way he could understand. "Besides, when lions are small, they're about as big as a cat, but they grow to be that big. Do you want to have to feed him out of your allowance?"

Peter shook his head. "Maybe I can get a kitty cat instead."

"Good thinking," Chase said as Jerrod approached, his expression thunderous. "We were just talking about the lions, and Peter has decided he doesn't want one."

Jerrod seemed to snap back to the present. "Well, that's a relief." He took Peter's hand, and they continued down the path, his walk rigid. "It seems our friend has been very worried and watching his back. But he thinks that another friend is behind all this."

"The other guy you fired?" Chase asked.

"Gary, and he isn't sure. But he says that he thinks he's being followed sometimes, and he's been getting strange phone calls—not nice ones." Chase figured Jerrod was talking vaguely so Peter wouldn't get upset.

"Daddy, look," Peter said, pointing to a huge lollipop, his eyes wide with wonder. "Can I have one?"

"Maybe a smaller one," Jerrod said just as Peter bounced with excitement.

"Peter, I'll buy you one that size," Chase said, pointing to one that wasn't too huge. "You go decide what flavor you want, and your daddy and I will help you get one. Okay?" Peter hurried to the cart to look, and Chase turned to Jerrod. "We have about two minutes."

"Steve is really scared. He's seen Gary around a few times with a woman. It's all he was able to tell me. But Steve said that Gary always had an interest in devices and building things. He didn't have time to go into anything more, but I think when we get back, we need to tell Red. Though I'm sure he's aware of the guy."

"Yeah. But each piece of information might help. We've looked at just about everyone at this point, and maybe all it will take is one bit of information for the pieces to fit together." Chase pulled out his phone and sent the info they had gotten to Red. He got an almost immediate acknowledgment saying that they were looking into it. "Okay. Let's leave them to do their job, and we can have some fun."

"I like the sound of that."

"I want a cherry one," Peter said as he raced back to them. Chase went to the cart and helped him get his treat. "Can I eat it now?"

"How about I take it to the truck and we put it aside until you get home? We don't want to get dirt on it."

Peter sighed. "Okay."

Chase paid for it and ran out to the truck. He put the lollipop where it would stay cool and then returned, showing his ticket for reentry. "Are you ready to go?" It seemed by their smiles that they both were.

PETER WAS half asleep by the time they got him into the house. They had had hot dogs, seen everything, ridden the safari tour, and practiced animal sounds until Chase's throat hurt. Jerrod put Peter on the sofa, and he dozed off almost immediately. "Where does he get all that energy?"

Jerrod chuckled. "Just wait. He'll rest for half an hour and then he'll be raring to go again." He went to the kitchen, and Chase followed him. "I'm going to brew some coffee. Do you want some too?"

"That would be nice." Chase sat at the table. "It was a fun day today."

"It was, and I think I needed that." Jerrod started the pot and sat down across from him. "I've been feeling really overwhelmed these past few days. And I keep wondering what's going to happen next. Though if I can survive Gizelle deciding to take Peter to the movies, I suppose I can live through anything." The coffee hissed as it brewed, the room filling with the roasted scent. Jerrod took Chase's hand, and they sat quietly until a knock on the door made them jump.

"Do you want me to get it?" Chase offered.

"Every time that happens, I wonder what's going to happen next," Jerrod admitted, and Chase went to answer the knock.

He opened the door partway. "Can I help you?"

"I need to speak to Jerrod," the man said breathlessly. Chase had no idea who it was, and he stayed in the doorway as Jerrod came up behind him.

"What do you want?" Jerrod asked harshly. "You need to leave."

The man's expression shifted from harried to threatening in a split second. "You need to listen to what I have to say."

"No, he doesn't," Chase added. "But you need to leave." Who in the hell was this guy anyway? He turned toward Jerrod, and as he did, the man pushed at Chase, nearly knocking him down, but he recovered and blocked the guy from getting inside. "Call the police," Chase snapped without taking his eyes off the potential intruder.

"I am," Jerrod said from behind him, and the guy turned and ran off down the sidewalk.

"Who was that?"

"Gary Lutz."

Chase hurried to the door and outside, pulling out his phone as he went. The call to Red went to voicemail. He left a message with the license plate and make of the car he was driving. He also relayed that he seemed to have threatened Jerrod. Once the black Toyota was gone, he returned and closed the door, locking it behind him.

"What the hell was he thinking?" Chase asked as he held Jerrod tightly. "Oh God. That guy tried to get in here."

"I know." Jerrod held Chase in return. "Damn, I'm glad you're strong and fast." Jerrod pulled away and lightly stroked Peter's head, which woke him. "Why can't anything just settle down? I'm an electrician, but lately every bit of drama in this town seems to center on me."

"And your sister-in-law," Chase said to himself. "Do you have this Steve's number? If not, get it. I have a question to ask him."

"Huh…?"

"You said that Steve saw Gary around town with a woman." He approached Jerrod, whose eyes widened.

"No way." But Chase nodded slowly. "Holy crap. You think Gizelle is involved in all of this?"

"Let's not jump to conclusions. I'd like to see what he has to say."

Jerrod left the room and returned with a number. Chase dialed it and waited. "Hello."

"This is a friend of Jerrod's," Chase said.

"I'm going to hang up."

"Don't. I think we may be able to help each other end this… all of it. Gary just paid us a visit and tried to get inside. The guy seemed a little crazy."

Steve breathed deeply enough the phone hummed. "He is."

Chase figured he'd take his shot. "You said you saw him with a woman. What did she look like?"

"I don't know. Middle height, with straight blond hair that was probably colored at one time. She looked kind of ragged. I guess if I think about it, her clothes were ruffled, and she carried this huge old-lady handbag." Chase found himself nodding, but Steve didn't stop there. "She had this mark on her neck, like a pink smudge." He paused. "Why is this important?"

"Because I think I might know who she is," Chase answered. "Thank you. Maybe we can bring this thing to an end for all of us." He ended the call.

"It was her?"

Chase nodded. "I'm sure of it."

"Do you think she really knows anything?" Jerrod asked.

"I don't know. But I think we might be finally unraveling all of this." At least he sure as hell hoped so.

CHAPTER 18

JERROD REMAINED quiet, not wanting to ask too many questions in front of Peter. Instead, they watched some cartoons for a while until Peter raced upstairs. "How do you think Gizelle is involved? How can she be?"

"I don't know. Except maybe she, Gary, and the construction company all had the same goal, or at least pieces of it." Chase grew quiet. "Let's talk this out. The construction company wanted everyone associated with AR out of the way. They contact someone local, maybe Gary, who likes to build devices and probably has firebug tendencies, to make things difficult. Maybe he sets a few fires, and maybe he meets Gizelle, who he finds out just happens to have a grudge against one of the people he wants to put pressure on. So maybe Gizelle gave him information or even money. You being homeless works into her plan to try to get Peter back."

"Okay. I can see that, even if it is a stretch."

"But maybe it isn't. Gary needs to get on the construction site to set the fire. Maybe Gizelle helps him there too," Chase offered. "All it would take is some distraction of security. The device gets planted, and up go the supplies. That only puts more pressure on you, which makes Gizelle happy."

"So the more pressure that gets put on me, the more Gizelle shows up and adds her own level of hell." It was starting to make sense, even if it was conjecture. "We know it's likely that Gary and Gizelle knew each other."

Chase nodded. "And Gizelle is just crazy enough and desperate enough to think that she could use your hardship to her advantage."

"But how do we prove any of this? It seems farfetched to me, though I know that Gizelle is crazy."

"I guess it all hinges on finding Gary and being able to place him at the fires."

Jerrod nodded. "We should tell the police. They should be able to look into things and put the pieces together?"

"I would think so. But maybe we can check in with Red tomorrow, let him know what we have so he has all the information. Then maybe he can find Gary and have more ammunition to use against Gizelle. She may be crazy, but she isn't insane, just incredibly selfish and off her rocker."

Peter's footsteps on the stairs were their cue to change the subject. "Can I eat my lollipop now?" he asked.

"Maybe some of it," Jerrod agreed. "But you can't have it all. It will give you a tummy ache, and that much sugar will have you up all night." Which was the last thing he needed. "I could break a piece off for you." Peter waited as Jerrod got him a piece, and then he went off to eat it. "Don't make a sticky mess everywhere."

"Okay, Daddy," Peter called, and Jerrod could just imagine cleaning sticky fingerprints off of everything. Still, Peter was happy, and judging by the way Chase was looking at him, Chase was happy too. Come to think of it, Jerrod was probably more content than he had a right to be.

"What do you want to do this evening?" Jerrod asked just as Chase's phone rang. He answered it, already hurrying toward the door. "A fire?"

"Yeah. I've got to go." Chase kissed him quickly, lingering a moment with a "damn," and then he was gone.

"Where'd Mr. Chase go?"

"He had to hurry to work," Jerrod said, hoping he would be okay as he hugged Peter. Chase had quickly become a very important part of his life, and now he couldn't help worrying that something would happen to him. The one bright spot over these past few weeks, other than that Peter was safe, had been Chase coming into his life. Jerrod took a deep breath, telling himself he was not going to worry. This was Chase's job, and he was damned good at it. Jerrod needed to remember that Chase could look after himself just like he looked after them. Still, he couldn't help worrying after all the goings-on over the past few weeks.

Jerrod got out his computer and checked for local news stories about a fire in town, but there was nothing. That didn't mean there wasn't a fire, just that it hadn't been written about yet. Still, he refused to sit here and worry all evening long. In the end, Jerrod ended up cleaning the kitchen and living room to keep himself busy and then tumbled into bed before midnight, exhausted.

JERROD WOKE alone and sighed. He had hoped that Chase might have joined him, but then he realized that he had never given him a key. Even if Chase had wanted to join him, he wouldn't have been able to do it without waking the entire house, and Chase would never do that. He was too thoughtful. Blinking himself fully awake, Jerrod grabbed his phone, where he found a message from Chase saying that he was okay and that he had gone home to sleep.

"Daddy," Peter said from the doorway before taking a running leap onto the bed.

"Morning, buddy," Jerrod said with a smile.

"Are you staying home like yesterday?" He had that cute, hopeful smile.

"I have to go to work, so you're going to the Y." He'd made sure that their procedures for picking up kids were tightened severely. At first he hadn't wanted Peter to go back, but they assured him that only he would be able to pick up Peter and no one else.

Peter nodded and bounced on the bed. "Can I go to the movies again?"

"No. But we can go to the movies together sometime soon. How would you like that?" He got out of bed and carried Peter toward his room. "We can get popcorn and even soda to drink."

"But not off the floor?" Peter asked.

Jerrod shivered as he thought of what Gizelle had done. "Right. Definitely not floor popcorn. Yuck." He made a face, and Peter did as well. After setting him down, Jerrod got Peter in the tub for a quick bath and then left him to dress. Then he made breakfast and managed to get them out of the house on time and dropped off Peter. He texted Chase that he was heading for his first job of the day before putting the truck in gear and heading to Mr. Dunston's to look into some wiring that seemed to be shorting out in his basement man cave.

"Morning," Mr. Dunston said as he came out of the house to shake Jerrod's hand. "Thanks for coming so quickly."

"No problem." He followed him inside and down to the basement, where Mr. Dunston showed him the problem.

"I need to go into the office, and Jean is out already, so take care of what you need to and lock the door behind you when you go." Wow, he hadn't expected that. "By the way, Jean loved her birthday present, and I even got the right color." He was all smiles as he practically leapt up the stairs, and Jerrod opened his toolbox and pulled out a power meter so he could begin to trace the source of the problem.

At first he thought it might be one of the outlets, but that wasn't it. They were all fine. He checked the breakers as well, but there was nothing there. Finally he checked a couple of the junction panels. Sure enough, some of the wiring insulation had been chewed away. Jerrod messaged Mr. Dunston about the issue and got a response that he would have the area treated right away. Mice would chew through anything, and in this case, they'd munched just enough of the wiring to cause an issue. Thankfully it was a run that went between two outlets, so Jerrod turned off the power and set to work running a new piece along through the basement wall.

Footsteps above caught his attention. "Mr. Dunston? Mrs. Dunston?" he called, coming to the bottom of the stairs. There was no further sound, and Jerrod thought he might have imagined it. Houses made sounds all the time. The house was quiet again, so he went back to work, getting the old wiring removed and the new line installed.

He stopped at another creak upstairs but continued with his work until a sound made him turn. "What the fuck are you doing here?" Jerrod asked when Gary reached the last step at the bottom of the stairs.

"I came to see you." His stare was as dark and black as night.

"Get out of here," Jerrod said, standing as tall and threatening as he could, though he wasn't built like Chase.

"Why? The owners aren't home. We're the only ones here." He smiled without a hint of warmth.

"What do you want?" Jerrod asked, fear rising, but he refused to give in to it.

"Your phone for a start," Gary said, holding out his hand. "And don't think about trying anything." He lifted a purple cloth grocery bag. "I brought a little present with me, and I can make it go off any time I want." He set it on the floor and backed away. "Now, give me your phone."

Jerrod slowly put his hand in his pocket, trying to think of a way he could signal for help, but he was trapped. As he reached for it, Chase's ring tone began to chime. Gary grabbed for the phone. "I have to answer it or he'll know something is wrong, and Chase knows where I am." God, he hoped Gary bought that lie. Before he could get an answer, Jerrod pressed the green button, watching Gary like a hawk.

"Sorry I missed you last night," Chase said. "I figured you and Peter were asleep and I didn't want to wake you."

Jerrod knew he had just seconds to try to tell Chase that he needed him and where he was. "It's okay. I had a job at Dunston's this morning." Gary tensed, and Jerrod shrugged. "It's going well. I have some help today, and that's making the job go much faster."

"Who?" Chase asked quickly.

Gary looked like he was about ready to explode, and Jerrod didn't want to push him any further. "I have to go. I'll talk to you later." He ended the call, and Gary snatched the phone out of his hand, dropped it to the concrete floor, and smashed it under his heel.

"That wasn't very smart."

"He's aware of my schedule, so he knows where I'm supposed to be," Jerrod lied. "Now what the heck is going on?"

"Isn't it obvious? You made a real mistake while making the repairs, and it started a fire that caught you by surprise. Now sit in that chair." He pulled plastic zip ties from his pocket, and once Jerrod sat down, he bound his wrists to the arms of the chair tightly enough that he couldn't move them.

"But why are you doing this?" Jerrod asked.

"To make you pay, of course. After you fired me, word got around that I wasn't very good, and I couldn't get a job for shit. I spent weeks sitting at home, and then some friends told me that Connor Warfield was looking for some help. They were looking for a way to get their foot in on the deal at the condos, and I was looking for a way to get even with you. It was a twofer. I got you sidelined—or so I thought—then I had to get AR out of the picture. They were paying me a lot." That much they had figured out, and it felt sort of good that he and Chase had been right, but shit, this was not how he wanted to find out. Jerrod hoped like hell that someone got here soon or there wasn't going to be much for them to find. "You ruined me. My wife left me after she heard what happened and took my kids. I needed cash, and Connor Warfield was willing to pay plenty to have their way cleared."

"What about Gizelle?" Jerrod asked.

Gary rolled his eyes as he placed the bag a few feet from where Jerrod sat. "That bitch? She was totally useless. I never told her about shit. She did have keys to your house, though, and apparently you piss off a lot of people, because she just gave them to me. Posing as the gas man was just a way to make sure the neighbors didn't take notice and made thing even easier. Too bad you weren't home when the fire started." The venom in his voice chilled Jerrod even more. "But you will be here." He turned and headed toward the stairs as sirens sounded in the distance, growing louder by the second. "What did you do?"

Jerrod shrugged as the sirens grew even louder. "I don't think you're going anywhere either, so you can either give up or burn down here right along with me. I'd say that's both the fire department and the police." He waited as Gary paled and hurried up the stairs, then closed the door at the top.

Jerrod turned to the purple bag, wondering what was going to happen. Multiple footsteps echoed through the house, people spreading out. "I'm down here." He hoped they found him before that damned thing went off. "Chase!"

"Jerrod?" Chase asked, opening the door at the top of the stairs.

"It's me. There's one of those damned devices down here. I don't know when it's going to go off." Chase hurried down and went to the laundry area to run water. Then he hurried in, grabbed the bag, and took it to the other room.

"The damned things short out when you get them wet," Chase explained as he returned, the water still running as he crouched down next to Jerrod and cut away the plastic straps. "Are you okay?"

"Yeah," Jerrod said, surrounded by Chase's big arms just as soon as he was free. "I'm fine, but he scared the shit out of me." Now that the danger was over, Jerrod clutched Chase hard, shaking like a leaf. He had been fine while it was going on, but now all he wanted to do was fly into a million pieces.

"Good. When you said you had help, I knew there was something wrong. All I could think about the entire way over was what I was going to do to that asshole if he hurt you." Chase held him tighter as police and other firefighters joined them. Jerrod let them take care of whatever Gary had intended to use to start the fire.

"We have someone in custody," Red said. "He was trying to get out through the backyard."

"Thank God," was all Jerrod could manage to say as he slumped into Chase's arms, closing his eyes. "At least this is finally over. Gary Lutz was the one who set the fires. He told me so himself. My sister-in-law did give him the keys to my house." Whatever that made her was up to the police.

"We'll get to the bottom of this now that he's in custody." Red seemed relaxed, but Jerrod was still shaking. He wanted to say that it would have been nice if they had gotten to the bottom of this whole thing a while ago, before some psycho broke into one of his jobs and threatened to burn him alive.

"Hey," Chase said softly. "It's over. They have the arsonist." The light touch on his chin had him lift his gaze to find Chase's shining back. "I was so scared the entire way over here. But it made me realize something."

"What?" Jerrod asked.

"How important you are to me. When I got your phone call, I could barely breathe. I knew you were in danger. I told the chief, who scrambled the entire department. We got the police, and the whole time over here, all I could do was pray that you were okay. The thought of anything happening to you scared me to death."

"That's because you're my hero."

Chase shook his head. "No. I'm not, I'm the guy who's fallen in love with you." Jerrod's breath hitched involuntarily, and he tried to find words. His lips even moved, but nothing came out. "I mean it. I love you, Jerrod, and I love Peter too. I know that it's a lot to ask to be part of your family, but I hope—"

Jerrod cut Chase off with a kiss right there. To think they were doing this in the Dunstons' basement was kind of weird, but at that moment, Jerrod didn't care. He held Chase with everything he had, his heart threatening to burst.

"Are you okay?" Chase asked once Jerrod pulled back. "Did I say something wrong?"

Somehow Jerrod found his voice. "Of course not," he croaked out. "I think I've been in love with you almost from the moment you rescued Peter. I have no idea why, but you've been there for us all through this. Most people would have run for the hills, but you were always there, even when I was a complete wreck." Maybe that was the very definition of love—seeing people at their worst and caring about them anyway. Jerrod looked around. "Do you think that maybe we can get out of this basement? Half the fire department is watching us."

Chase turned around to take in the six huge guys all staring at them. "What? Have you never seen two people say they love each other?"

One of the guys rolled his eyes. "Oh please. We've been waiting for you to say something for a week now. You've been completely twitterpated the entire time. Maybe now you won't spend your entire days with stars in your eyes."

"Look who's talking," Chase retorted.

"Yeah. I think Hayden was worse when he met Kyle," one of the guys said.

"All right, get back to work." That must have been Hayden. "We need to get the device secured."

"And I need to get back to the station. Technically I'm still on duty." Chase pulled away. "And I don't think the department is going to be particularly happy about me kissing you while I'm on the clock." His arms slipped away, and Jerrod missed them immediately. "Are you going to be okay to get home?"

"Yes. I'll be fine." And he knew he would be. "You be careful, and I'll see you back at the house." Jerrod still had work to finish, and he was going to have one hell of a time explaining to Mr. and Mrs. Dunston everything that had happened in their basement.

"Are you sure? I can follow you home."

Jerrod nodded. "I'm fine. I can breathe again, and I have work to do the same as you."

"All right. The guys have the shorted-out device, and we're all going to head out. I'm sure the police will have questions for you." He smiled, and all the firefighters left the basement.

Red came down the stairs, and all Jerrod could do was wait nervously for answers.

"You have Gary, right?"

"Yes," Red answered. "He's in a car on his way to the county jail."

"Look, I need to get this work done, and Mr. and Mrs. Dunston are going to flip when they find out that half the police and fire departments have been through their house."

"Don't worry. Mrs. Dunston is upstairs. She got home ten minutes ago, and everything has been explained. There's nothing for you to worry about. She's even made some coffee and offered her kitchen table as a place for us to talk."

Jerrod supposed that it was inevitable that he would need to relive what happened multiple times, so he might as well get this over with. He put his tools in the box and followed Red up the stairs. "Let the questioning begin."

It had been one hell of a day by the time he got Peter from the Y and returned home. Chase met them both at the door, and Peter ran up to him for a hug.

"Are you going to live here with us?" Peter asked.

Chase seemed surprised. "Well...."

"Why do you ask?" Jerrod spoke up to rescue Chase, whose cheeks were turning redder by the second.

"Mr. Chase is here all the time, and he sleeps with you in your bed. So I thought that he was going to live here too." Peter went inside, leaving Chase blinking at him.

"Sometimes that kid sees way too much," Chase said with a smile forming at the edges of his lips.

"Yeah, he does, although...."

"Hey. Things between us are new," Chase said. "You and I don't need to make a bunch of rush decisions all of a sudden."

Jerrod nodded. "Do you not want to live here with us?" He had no idea why he asked. They had known each other only a few weeks, and it was too soon for that.

"Of course I want to. But maybe you and I can date like normal people for a while, go to dinner, the movies—you know, normal things, rather than chasing arsonists and dealing with crazy sisters-in-law."

"Maybe hiking in the woods?" Jerrod asked. "I really want Peter to experience things outside of town."

Chase chuckled. "We could go camping, if you like. I used to do things like that when I was a teenager with the Boy Scouts."

Jerrod chuckled. "I should have known."

"That I was a Boy Scout? I'll have you know that I was an Eagle Scout by the time I was seventeen." He puffed his chest out.

"Of course you were. You're still a Boy Scout now. My Boy Scout," Jerrod whispered before kissing Chase gently. "And yes, I'd love to go camping, roast marshmallows, and sit around the campfire singing songs and stuff. Johnny loved the outdoors."

"Then we'll do things like that. I have sleeping bags somewhere that will zip together, so we can keep each other warm on cold nights."

"Are we going camping?" Peter asked.

"Do you want to go?" Chase asked. "Your daddy and I could take you camping some weekend yet this summer if you want to go."

Peter ran around the room and then did this butt-wiggling dance that clearly showed he was happy. "I'm going to go pack." He ran up the stairs, and Jerrod pulled away from Chase, chuckling.

"I think that's a yes." Damn, did he dare hope there would be many more yeses in their future?

CHAPTER 19

IT TOOK a few weeks, but Chase got an entire weekend off and a tent camping site reservation out at Pine Grove Furnace State Park. Ever since he'd gotten confirmation of the reservation and told Peter and Jerrod, Peter had had his bags packed and was all ready to go. Chase had borrowed a tent large enough for the three of them, with a little extra room in case they needed it. He'd also gotten a canopy to cover the picnic table in case it rained.

"Are you ready to go?" Chase asked as Jerrod let him inside. He'd come right from his Friday shift.

"Yes, yes, yes!" Peter bounded over, pulling his BB8 suitcase behind him.

Jerrod rolled his eyes. "He's been ready for days. I have a cooler packed and a bag of things I'm going to need."

"Then let's get everything into the truck and we can go. It's supposed to be a sunny weekend, and there are places that we can all go hiking and swimming and stuff." Chase was excited too. The truck already had all the equipment stowed, so once he got Jerrod's cooler and their bags loaded, they locked up the house and headed south out of town.

"How long will it take to get there?" Peter asked.

"Not long. But you can count cows along the way," Chase offered, figuring they would need something to keep Peter busy.

"Horses instead," Peter countered, and they all counted the horses they saw until they reached the woods. They pulled into the campground and found their site, which was plenty big enough and even close to the bathrooms.

"Do you want to help put up the tent?" Chase asked Peter, and he hurried after him. Jerrod started setting up the canopy for over the picnic table, so Chase unrolled the tent and had Peter hand him the poles. Once they were in the sleeves, Peter held one side as Chase got the poles arched and the tent up and staked. "You were a really big help." It probably took longer than if Chase had done it on his own, but Peter was so pleased, and part of this trip was to make things fun for him.

"Can we make a fire?" Peter asked.

"Later," Jerrod told him. "Why don't you get your sleeping bag and suitcase in the tent." Giving Peter jobs to do kept him busy and made him part of the process.

By the time they had everything up and the beds all set, it was getting dark. Chase built a fire and brought out the hot dog sticks, helping Peter with his as Jerrod set up the table for dinner.

"Do you want some music?" Jerrod asked, setting a radio on the table. It had probably been his since he was a kid. He turned it on soft enough so it didn't disturb the other sites. It was an oldies station, and Chase settled in to enjoy the evening and the company.

"The construction firm of Connor Warfield has been indicted"— Jerrod turned up the story—"on racketeering charges in conjunction with a number of local individuals involving a bid to muscle into the northside condominium project in Carlisle. A company spokesman had no comment, and the names of the local individuals involved have not yet been released by police. A spokesperson for AR Construction, the current contractor, has said that the project will continue and that they are suing Connor Warfield for damages related to a fire at the construction site. We will update you with details as more become available." The music began once more, and Jerrod sat next to him, bumping Chase's shoulder.

"It really does seem like it's finally over. Mr. Dunston's office called today, and they have gotten everything cleared with the insurance company. A payoff has been arranged, and once my mortgage is settled, I will be receiving a sizable check that I can use to buy a new home for Peter and me. Then we'll be able to have a home of our own once more."

"I see." Chase was happy that Jerrod could move on with his life.

Jerrod bumped his shoulder. "I was thinking that once all this is settled, maybe you and I could go house hunting and find a place that we all like. Somewhere with a yard where Peter can have a swing set of his own.

"Can I get a cat?" Peter asked.

"Yes, you can. Once we get a new house, you can get a pet if you want." Jerrod leaned against Chase, and Chase put an arm around him, content and damned happy.

"Really?" Peter asked.

"Yes. But we have to wait until we get our new house and are moved in. Then we'll talk about what you want." Jerrod sighed and helped Peter get his hot dog made the way he liked it with ketchup and pickles. Chase slipped away with a couple of hot dogs and returned a little while later with one for each of them.

"This is the best way to make these," Chase said, and soon they were all seated at the table. "Tomorrow, I thought I'd make eggs and bacon over the fire."

"Yummy," Peter said, taking a bite. Chase had no idea if it was for the eggs and bacon or the hot dog, but he was happy, and it seemed the rest of them were too.

"Another?" Chase asked Jerrod, and he ended up making a second for both of them.

Darkness descended. Jerrod set a battery lamp on the table until they finished eating. Then Chase set up the chairs around the fire, with Peter climbing into Chase's lap.

"Tell stories," Peter said.

"What kind of story?" Chase asked. "Wait, I know. I heard one about a man who came upon a fire in the woods at night. He was cold, and it looked warm, but when he got close enough, he found that it wasn't a fire at all, but a dragon." Chase growled, and Peter giggled. "The dragon was really warm, and he shot fire at the man, but he hid behind a rock and the fire went around him. Still, the dragon roared, and the man peeked out and saw that the dragon had stepped into a trap and that his leg was hurting."

Peter's eyes were huge. "What happened?"

"The man asked if the dragon would let him get the trap off without burning him up, and the dragon said yes."

"Wow. Daddy, I want a dragon for a pet," Peter said, making them both chuckle.

"Anyway," Chase interrupted, "the man crept out and slowly moved closer. Then he pulled at the trap and opened it so the dragon could get his foot free. Then he wrapped it in a bandage, and the dragon limped away a little ways. Then he spread his wings, and the air all around felt like a mighty wind. The dragon lifted off the ground and flew up, up, and away, getting smaller and smaller until he disappeared from sight."

Peter turned to look at him. "Is that it? Where did the dragon go? Didn't he say thank you or let the man ride on his back?" Peter crossed his arms over his chest. "The dragon was mean."

"No. The dragon had to go home so he could help the mama dragon and the baby dragons that depended on him."

"Oh." Peter stared at him. "I think you need to be able to tell better stories."

Jerrod was biting his lower lip as Chase looked at him. "Okay, then. Maybe next time Daddy can tell you the story."

Peter grew quiet. "No. I like the story, just make it better next time."

"So you want there to be a next time?" Chase asked.

Peter nodded. "I liked the dragon part." Was a six-year-old throwing him a bone? Chase almost laughed. He had never been a good storyteller, but that was okay. Peter yawned and leaned back against him. Story or not, Chase found it strange the way Peter had taken to him. Chase didn't want to step on Jerrod's toes, but he liked that Peter seemed to have accepted him.

"How about I help you get ready for bed? We have a big day tomorrow, and you're going to want to be ready for it." Jerrod lifted Peter into his arms and placed him on his feet before leading him up to the bathrooms. Chase sat alone near the fire, the dark woods around them muffling the sounds of the other campers, like occasional laughter, or the shuffling of someone as they passed on the road. He leaned back, closing his eyes, letting the sounds of the night lull him into a relaxed daze until Peter and Jerrod returned.

Chase said good night to Peter, and Jerrod took him off to bed, returning a few minutes later. "He's already out. I wish I could fall asleep that quickly."

"Me too," Chase agreed and pulled a chair next to him for Jerrod. "We could talk if you want."

Jerrod sighed. "You know, I think I'm a little talked out. The police were by a couple times this week asking questions and going over things again. Gizelle is fighting the charges against her, trying to say that it was some kind of misunderstanding. That isn't going to fly, but they need as much information as possible." He slowly sat down, and Chase took his hand. Sometimes it seemed like the drama around her would never die down.

"Yeah, I get it. Every call I go on has me wondering if our arsonist is on the loose again. I know he isn't, but I keep wondering and looking for him. But one good thing did come out of this. Hayden has asked me to work with him as a fire marshal. He says I have good instincts." Chase didn't particularly like the idea that part of the reason he was getting this opportunity was because of Jerrod and Peter's troubles, but then he kept telling himself that he helped bring them to a close.

"It's sure quiet out here," Jerrod said in a whisper. "I don't want to talk too loudly in case I disturb things."

"I know." Chase looked up at the stars that had appeared between the branches of the trees. The fire had burned down, and Chase thought about putting another log on, but decided against it. "Maybe we should get some rest too. I have an idea that Peter is going to be up early and raring to go."

Jerrod chuckled, and Chase stirred the embers before heading over to the bathroom. By the time he returned, the fire was nearly out. Jerrod took his turn to clean up while Chase made sure everything was buttoned up for the night. Then he and Jerrod slipped into the tent and into the double sleeping bag as the cool night air settled around them. Peter was sound asleep, and as soon as Jerrod rolled onto his side, Chase snuggled up to him, slipping an arm around him. Jerrod chuckled softly.

"You know we can't do that," he whispered.

"I know. But just being next to you does that to me." He closed his eyes, and they both drifted off… eventually.

"Daddy, Mr. Chase," Peter said from next to him.

Chase cracked his eyes open. "What is it, buddy?"

"I gotta go," Peter said.

Chase slipped out of the sleeping bag and pulled light sweatpants over his sleep shorts and then put on a T-shirt. He slipped on his shoes.

"You need shoes," Chase said, and Peter got his on, and then, as quietly as he could, Chase took Peter to the bathroom, which was crowded as the campground began to wake. While Peter went, Chase slapped some cold water on his face, stifling a yawn. Then he let Peter use the sink to wash his hands before they walked back to their site.

"Is Daddy awake?" Peter asked.

"I think he's really tired, so can you be quiet and get dressed without saying anything and waking him? Then you and me can go for a walk and let your daddy sleep." He tried to make it sound important, and Peter nodded solemnly before going into the tent. He came out five minutes later, and Chase helped him with his shoes. "We can go for a walk if you want," Chase whispered.

"I'm awake," Jerrod groaned from inside, and after some moving and even an under-his-breath cuss, Jerrod climbed out of the tent.

"Come on, Daddy. There's lots to see," Peter said.

"Let Chase get dressed, and then we can go," Jerrod said, and Chase hurriedly dressed properly before joining the other two.

Peter had a huge amount of energy and kept running ahead and then coming back. "Did you rest well?" Chase asked quietly. "I tried to get Peter to let you sleep."

Jerrod smiled. "He didn't say a word, but he put his suitcase on my feet." He snickered. "Doesn't matter. I needed to get up." He bumped Chase's shoulder. "Thanks for getting up with him."

"Daddy!" Peter cried, running over as they approached the main road. "Look. Ponies." He jumped up and down.

Chase went over to the trailer, where small heads poked out the back to see what was going on. "Hello."

"Hey," the driver said.

"Are you giving rides?" Chase asked.

"Yes. We're about to set up near the meadow. Hopefully we'll be open in an hour."

"Can we sign up or something?" Chase asked, and the driver nodded, taking Chase's name and giving him a ten o'clock time for Peter. Chase put down a deposit and returned to where Peter could barely contain himself. "He can go for a ride at ten."

"Really?" Peter asked.

"Yes, really. But we should get breakfast before we do anything else." Chase smiled as Peter skipped almost the entire way back to the campsite.

"Is it a nice pony?" Peter asked, holding Jerrod's hand as they approached the makeshift pen. He was still excited, but his caution seemed to have welled up.

"Yes. All my ponies are really nice," the man said as he gave Peter a carrot. "Hold your hand flat and she'll take it from you." Peter slowly extended his hand, and the pony took the carrot with her lips and then crunched it. "Is that the one you want to ride?" he asked, and Peter nodded.

"She's pretty."

"Okay. Let's get you all set." Chase paid the rest of the money while Jerrod filled out the forms. The man helped Peter get on a helmet before lifting him onto the back of the pony. "Hold on right here." He showed Peter, and then he led the pony out of the enclosure and along the edge of the meadow.

"Now that's something," Jerrod said as Peter rode in a large circle through the area. He was never more than twenty-five or so yards away, but once they turned back, Chase could see Peter's grin.

"Can I have a pony?" Peter asked.

"I don't think so. Where would we keep it? Your bed would be too small." Jerrod grinned back, and Chase slipped an arm around his waist while one of the pony attendants led Peter around the circle a second time. "Thank you for this… for everything," Jerrod said softly.

Chase grinned and leaned his head against Jerrod's. "I was going to say the same thing to you. This, the three of us…." He didn't have the words for how he felt, other than love, pure and simple love.

"I know. It's like something just fell into place that I wasn't looking for." Jerrod turned to him, and Chase knew exactly what he meant. He felt the same way. They watched as Peter's ride came to an end.

"Do you want a picture?" the attendant asked.

"Yes," Jerrod said, leaving Peter on the pony, standing just in front. Chase was about to use his phone to snap the image.

"I can take some of all of you," the attendant said, and Chase stood next to Jerrod, smiling at the camera. Jerrod slipped an arm through his, the three of them smiled, and even the pony seemed happy, lifting her head to look into the lens. The sun was perfect, the breeze tousling Peter's hair—a moment of perfection. Chase didn't realize it at the time, but that image on his phone would be the first of many family pictures.

EPILOGUE

CHASE CLIMBED off the truck, completely wiped out after spending hours battling a blaze at a warehouse between Carlisle and Mechanicsburg. Every unit from the surrounding communities had been called in to try to bring the structure under control. In the end, with enough unknown chemicals in the building, it had taken hours in the heat and spray before they could get the fire out.

"What has you so excited?" Hayden asked as Chase jumped down off the truck.

"It's moving day, or at least it was," Chase answered. They had found a house in the Old Mooreland area of town. It had been built in the forties, with great bones, even if the interior was dated and needed work. There was a nice yard with a fence for Peter, and they had already arranged for the delivery of a play set. Chase intended to assemble it on his next day off.

"Did Jerrod get stuck with all of it?" Hayden asked.

"Pretty much. I got called in just as the truck pulled up at his rental. There isn't all that much still there, and hopefully the movers were helpful." He pulled off his gear, completely soaked to the skin with sweat, even with the chill in the fall air. "I'm hoping I can shower and get out of here." This was supposed to have been his day off, but duty called. He understood that, and so did Jerrod. Still, days like today were unfair.

"Go," Hayden told him. "Help your man get everything moved." He smiled as Chase hurried away and upstairs to the living area.

Chase grabbed his bag, showered, and dressed in clean clothes. Then he took off before anyone could find a reason for him to stay.

He made a call and a stop before pulling up in front of the house. The front door stood open, but the truck was nowhere to be found. "You missed all of it," Jerrod said as he came out the door. "They got everything loaded, unloaded, and brought inside pretty quickly."

"So it's all here?"

"Yes. All we have to do is get the last of your stuff out of your apartment in the next week and we'll be all moved in." Jerrod slipped his arms around Chase's neck. "I heard stories about the fire."

"Yeah, it was bad," Chase said, hugging Jerrod. "Where's Peter?"

"Out back," Jerrod said. "Were you able to get it?" Chase nodded and returned to the car to pick up a box from the floor of the front seat. By the time he returned, Jerrod had called Peter outside. "You've been so helpful with this move and everything that Chase and I got you something."

Chase opened the top of the box, and Peter gasped as a small ginger-striped kitten poked its head out.

Peter screamed with delight before gently lifting the kitten into his arms and holding him to his chest. "Is he really mine?"

"Yes. Your daddy and I arranged to get him for you. But you have to take care of him, feed him, and be gentle with him."

"Oh, I will." Peter smiled from ear to ear. "Let's go inside and I'll show you the house, and you can sleep in my bed and everything." He went inside, still talking to the kitten, and Chase stared after him.

"We have the house, the fence, and one kid," Chase said. "That's a lot more than I ever expected." He placed an arm around Jerrod as they headed inside. "I think I have just about everything I ever wanted."

"Yeah. I suppose anything is possible, and between the two of us, we can do just about anything."

"Yup. The two of us, Peter, and a cat. Though I still think a dog would be nice," Chase said as Peter ran out toward them and stopped at the door.

"Daddy, Peaches just peed in the kitchen," Peter cried.

Chase turned to Jerrod with a half smile. "Okay. Maybe we don't need the dog." He kissed Jerrod quickly and then followed him inside.

Keep reading for an excerpt from
Fire and Water
By Andrew Grey!

CHAPTER 1

RED MARKHAM heard the call for backup through the radio, flipped on the flashing lights of his patrol car, and took off down High Street. He turned north and drove two blocks, going through the stop sign as quickly as he could. Red pulled to a stop behind the other squad car and unfolded himself from the seat. He could see over the hood what the problem was and strode over to where two other officers were struggling with a suspect.

"Get the hell away from me. I wasn't doing nothing!" the suspect yelled at the top of his lungs, trying to yank his arm away from Smith. He managed it, too, and used the free hand to punch Rogers. "You have no right!" Smith got hold of him again. The guy wasn't that large, but he was hopped up on something, that was for sure. When Red caught sight of his eyes, they were as big as saucers, red, dilated, and as wild as a feral cat's.

"That's enough!" Red snapped, wielding his voice like a weapon. The suspect continued struggling.

"Tase him, for God's sake," Rogers called. Smith went for his stun gun, but the suspect knocked his hand away. The situation was turning dangerous fast. Red approached and pulled his weapon.

"Get down now!"

The suspect turned toward him and instantly stopped moving.

"I said get down on the ground!" Red's voice became sharper. Drill sergeants could take lessons from him, or so he'd been told.

The suspect's wide eyes got even bigger somehow, and he stilled completely. Then he dropped to the sidewalk on his stomach and didn't move. "What the hell are you?" the suspect asked under his breath.

Red ignored the comment and kept his gun on the guy while the other two officers cuffed him. Once the suspect was under control, Red put away his weapon.

"Jesus Christ, I'm in the middle of the freak patrol."

"That's plenty out of you," Smith told the prone suspect. "You already have more trouble than you can handle." Smith read him his rights and strongly advised him to keep his mouth shut for the foreseeable future. Red stepped back and glared at the suspect, making sure he made no move toward his fellow officers.

"What happened?" Red asked once the suspect was calm.

"Don't know. He looked strange, and when I stopped to see if he needed help, he went off," Rogers explained. He was a few years older than Red, and they'd joined the Carlisle police force at about the same time. Not that Red knew him all that well, outside of work, or Smith, for that matter. Both men were good guys who Red trusted to have his back when he needed it. But calling either of them friends was a stretch.

"The guy's higher than a kite," Smith chimed in.

"Some new stuff has hit town, and it's strong as hell. This is the second guy like this I've had to deal with, and the department's had about six so far. It's bad and getting worse," Rogers added.

The suspect wasn't moving, and Smith bent down. "Shit, call an ambulance. He's barely breathing."

Rogers radioed in, and within a minute they heard sirens approaching. That was the beauty of a town this size. The ambulance garage was only a mile away, and those guys were always on the ball. Red didn't take his eyes off the suspect in case he was playing possum, but he grew more and more limp. The ambulance arrived, and the EMTs took charge of the suspect, worked on him on the ground, and then got him on a gurney and into the ambulance. Rogers rode along, and Smith prepared to follow in their car, but it didn't look good to Red, not at all.

"Hey, man," Smith said just before they got ready to leave. "Appreciate the help." This whole situation had gone from bad to worse to possibly tragic within about two minutes.

"No problem. I'll see you back at the station." The back doors of the ambulance thunked closed, and Smith went to his car. Red waited until they all drove away before going to his. He sat in the driver's seat and adjusted his rearview mirror. He did not look at himself in it. He never looked in a mirror if he could help it. He knew what he looked like and didn't fucking need to be reminded. He was well aware he was never, ever going to win any beauty contests.

Red snapped out of his thoughts when he heard another call—an altercation at the Y. That was a new one. He responded to the call and was informed that an ambulance was already on its way, along with the fire department. What a fucking day. He wondered for two seconds if it was a full moon, but he didn't believe in all that crap anyway, so he flipped on his lights and hurried to his next call.

The Y was in an old school building that had been expanded. The old part was just that, old, while the addition was new, shiny, and well equipped. Red parked near the ambulance and rescue vehicles. He headed inside and was directed to the pool area. Not that he would have had any trouble figuring out where to go from all the people huddled outside the door. People loved to gawk. "Excuse me," Red said, and some of the people turned around. They stared, the way everyone seemed to stare, and silently got out of the way, tapping others on the shoulder, parting groups of people in workout gear and dripping bathing suits like the Red Sea.

Pushing through the door, Red took in the scene. A woman and a young man in a small red bathing suit stood off to the side. The woman, about thirty or so, Red guessed, soccer-mom type, was yelling and trying to poke the kid in the chest. One of the firemen was trying to separate them and looked grateful when Red approached.

"What's going on?" His voice echoed off the walls of the natatorium.

The woman stopped still, and the kid took a step back, nearly falling into the pool. "He…," the woman began, regaining her composure. "He nearly killed my son."

"I did not, lady," the kid protested, crossing his arms over his sculpted chest. Red quickly took him in and swallowed hard. He was a specimen of damn near perfect manhood, like he belonged on the cover of some magazine. He allowed the thought for a split second. "If you'd have been watching your son and making sure he obeyed the rules the way you're supposed to, none of this would have happened."

"All right. You, over there." Red pointed to the kid. "Sit down, and wait for me." Red then turned to the woman. "You, follow me." He took a step back and waited for both of them to obey his instructions. "Sit here, and I'll be with you in a minute." He waited for her to do as she was told and walked over to where a young boy lay on the tile around the pool. The kid was blue, and Red watched as two EMTs tried to resuscitate him. It didn't look good, but then the kid coughed, spit up water, and gasped for air. Red motioned to the woman, and she hurried over. The boy, who looked about eight, coughed again, and the paramedics told him to stay still. His mother rushed to him, and he began to cry.

"You're going to be all right," the paramedic said to him. Red had crossed paths with Arthur before and knew he knew his stuff. "Just rest and breathe."

"Mom," the kid said.

She took his hand. "You're all right," she soothed, and then she began thanking the people who'd helped her son.

"We're going to take him to the hospital so we can check him out," Arthur told the woman. She nodded and didn't release her son's hand.

"Ma'am, I need to speak with you," Red told her. She nodded and whispered to her son before getting up and walking over to where Red waited. "What happened?"

"I didn't see it. I had dropped Connor off for his swimming lesson, and he was going to stay for open swim afterwards. He and his friends usually do. I got here and saw them pulling him out of the water. I called the police." She turned toward the lifeguard, who sat where Red had told him to. He looked nervous as hell. "I only know that if he'd been doing his job, none of this would have happened," she spat.

Red pulled out his pad and began writing down what she had told him. He got her name, Mary Robinson. He also got her address, telephone number, her date of birth, along with Connor's, and all other pertinent information. "So just to be clear, you didn't see exactly what happened?"

"No, but…." Her argument had rung hollow, and it looked like it was starting to sound that way to her as well. She looked toward her son. Red noticed that she was looking anywhere other than at him. It was something he'd gotten used to.

"It's all right. We'll find out what happened."

She kept looking at her son, and Red stepped back to let her be with him. Then he walked over to where the lifeguard sat on the bottom row of a set of bleachers set up along the side of the pool so spectators could watch races.

Red saw the startled expression on the kid's face as he approached. The kid did a better job than most of covering the pity Red saw flash through his eyes for a split second. "Can you tell me your name, please?" Red asked, getting things moving.

"Terry Baumgartner," he answered, swallowing hard. "He and his friends were horsing around on the pool deck. I told them more than once to stop and was about to ask them to leave when I turned away because a little girl had approached my seat. And when I looked back, I saw him under the water. I dove in, along with Julie." He motioned to the young woman in a red one-piece swimsuit who stood a little ways away. "I reached him first and pulled him out. We started resuscitation right away and continued until we were relieved a few minutes later."

"Who called this in?" Red asked.

A man stepped forward. "I did. They yelled to call 911, so I did. The kids were roughhousing, and I remember thinking someone was going to get hurt."

"Daddy, is Connor going to be okay?" a little girl in a wet bathing suit asked as she walked up and took the man's hand.

"Yes, honey, he's going to be fine," he said, soothing the kid's fears before turning back to Red. He swallowed as he met Red's eyes. Very few people did that anymore. "What he said is the truth. The kids were asking for trouble. If the lifeguard did anything wrong, it was not kicking them out earlier. But he did warn them."

Red glanced to Terry, who nodded. Some of the worry seemed to slip from his aqua eyes, and his godlike, lanky body lost some of its tension. He lowered his lean arms and let them hang down from his sculpted shoulders. Damn—the kid wasn't big, but he was perfect, as far as Red was concerned. "Thank you," Red said, turning back to the man. He took down his contact information and asked a few more questions before thanking him again. He then talked to the other lifeguard, Julie, who confirmed what Terry had told him. Red was satisfied that this was an accident and that the lifeguard hadn't been responsible. He then spoke with the manager of the facility and got the necessary information from him. He was very helpful and seemed concerned and relieved at the same time.

By the time Red was done, Connor had been taken to the hospital, and most everyone else had been dismissed. He was getting ready to leave when he saw Terry and Julie standing off to one side, talking animatedly back and forth. Their voices weren't as quiet as he assumed they meant them to be, because he heard little snippets of their conversation. "I'd die if that happened to me," he heard Terry say and saw the kid looking his way. Red ignored him and walked carefully over the wet tile toward the door. Beauty was only skin deep.

"Red." He turned and saw Arthur approaching. He'd obviously heard what was being said as well. "Don't listen to them. That kid is as shallow as an overturned saucer." Arthur said it a little louder than necessary, and the chatter from the corner ceased abruptly. "When you get off tonight, you want to meet us at Hanover Grille?" he asked more softly. "Some of us are going to have some dinner and hang out for a while. You're welcome to join us, you know that."

Red smiled slightly. He was self-conscious about his smile, and when it threatened to go wider, he put his hand in front of his mouth. "Thanks." His impulse was to say no, thank you, and just go home after work, but Arthur was sincere, and it might be good to get out with people for a change. "Once I'm off shift and get my reports done, I'll try to stop by. It may be late, though."

"I know how things work," Arthur said, and then he hurried away, out of the natatorium.

Red did a mental check that he had spoken to everyone and had all the information he needed. He confirmed he had, and when he checked the clock on the wall, he said a silent thank-you and left the building.

As soon as he pushed open the outside door, he saw four news vans out front, with reporters milling around getting ready to file their stories. Red went right to his car and left, even as they were making their way over. He had no intention of making any comments to the press. He would head back to the station and let the powers that be decide who they wanted to speak for the department.

He got back to the station and filled in the captain about both the suspect on the sidewalk and the near drowning. He made sure the captain knew about the reporters and then headed to his desk to start writing reports. It took an hour. He filed them and got ready to leave. It had been a long, exciting day, and he was exhausted. Red didn't talk much with the other officers in the station. He did say good-bye to the ones he encountered, to be polite, and then hurried to leave.

Red was already in his car and pulling out of the lot when he remembered Arthur's invitation. Since he didn't have anything to do this evening besides sit at home, watch television, and drink too much beer, he decided to take Arthur up on his offer.

Scan the QR Code
Below to Order!

ANDREW GREY is the author of more than two hundred works of Contemporary Gay Romantic fiction, including an Amazon Editors Best Romance of 2023. After twenty-seven years in corporate America, he has now settled down in Central Pennsylvania with his husband of more than twenty-five years, Dominic, and his laptop. An interesting ménage. Andrew grew up in western Michigan with a father who loved to tell stories and a mother who loved to read them. Since then he has lived throughout the country and traveled throughout the world. He is a recipient of the RWA Centennial Award, has a master's degree from the University of Wisconsin–Milwaukee, and now writes full-time. Andrew's hobbies include collecting antiques, gardening, and leaving his dirty dishes anywhere but in the sink (particularly when writing). He considers himself blessed with an accepting family, fantastic friends, and the world's most supportive and loving partner. Andrew currently lives in beautiful, historic Carlisle, Pennsylvania.

Email:andrewgrey@comcast.net

Website:www.andrewgreybooks.com

Follow me on BookBub

THROUGH the FLAMES

ANDREW GREY

Carlisle
Fire

1

Kyle Wilson hasn't had it easy. His insecurities and nasty home life made him lash out as a kid, and when he finally came out as gay, his family disowned him. Then, just when he's pulled his life together and gotten his construction company running, he's caught in a fire and forced to take costly time off.

When firefighter Hayden Walters rescues a man from a burning building, he's just doing his job. He doesn't expect it to turn his life upside-down, but the man is none other than Hayden's high school bully.

He definitely doesn't expect Kyle to come to the station to thank him in person.

With awkward apologies out of the way, Kyle and Hayden realize they have a lot in common. And when it turns out someone set the fire at Kyle's construction site to target him, they find they can solve each other's problems too: Hayden needs a place to stay while his apartment is renovated, and Kyle doesn't want to be alone in case the firebug strikes again. Things between the two of them quickly heat up—but so does the arsonist's agenda. Can they track down the would-be killer before it's too late?

SCAN THE QR CODE
BELOW TO ORDER!

FIRE AND SAND
ANDREW GREY

Can a single dad with a criminal past find love with the cop who pulled him over?

When single dad Quinton Jackson gets stopped for speeding, he thinks he's lost both his freedom and his infant son, who's in the car he's been chasing down the highway. Amazingly, State Trooper Wyatt Nelson not only believes him, he radios for help and reunites Quinton with baby Callum.

Wyatt should ticket Quinton, but something makes him look past Quinton's record. Watching him with his child proves he made the right decision. Quinton is a loving, devoted father—and he's handsome. Wyatt can't help but take a personal interest.

For Quinton, getting temporary custody is a dream come true… or it would be, if working full-time and caring for an infant left time to sleep. As if that weren't enough, Callum's mother will do anything to get him back, including ruining Quinton's life. Fortunately, Quinton has Wyatt for help, support, and as much romance as a single parent can schedule.

But when Wyatt's duties as a cop conflict with Quinton's quest for permanent custody, their situation becomes precarious. Can they trust each other, and the courts, to deliver justice and a happy ever after?

SCAN THE QR CODE
BELOW TO ORDER!

ANDREW
GREY

HEARTWARD

He doesn't know that home is where his heart will be....

Firefighter Tyler Banik has seen his share of adventure while working disaster relief with the Red Cross. But now that he's adopted Abey, he's ready to leave the danger behind and put down roots. That means returning to his hometown—where the last thing he anticipates is falling for his high school nemesis.

Alan Pettaprin isn't the boy he used to be. As a business owner and council member, he's working hard to improve life in Scottville for everyone. Nobody is more surprised than Alan when Tyler returns, but he's glad. For him, it's a chance to set things right. Little does he guess he and Tyler will find the missing pieces of themselves in each other. Old rivalries are left in the ashes, passion burns bright, and the possibility for a future together stretches in front of them....

But not everyone in town is glad to see Tyler return....

SCAN THE QR CODE BELOW TO ORDER!

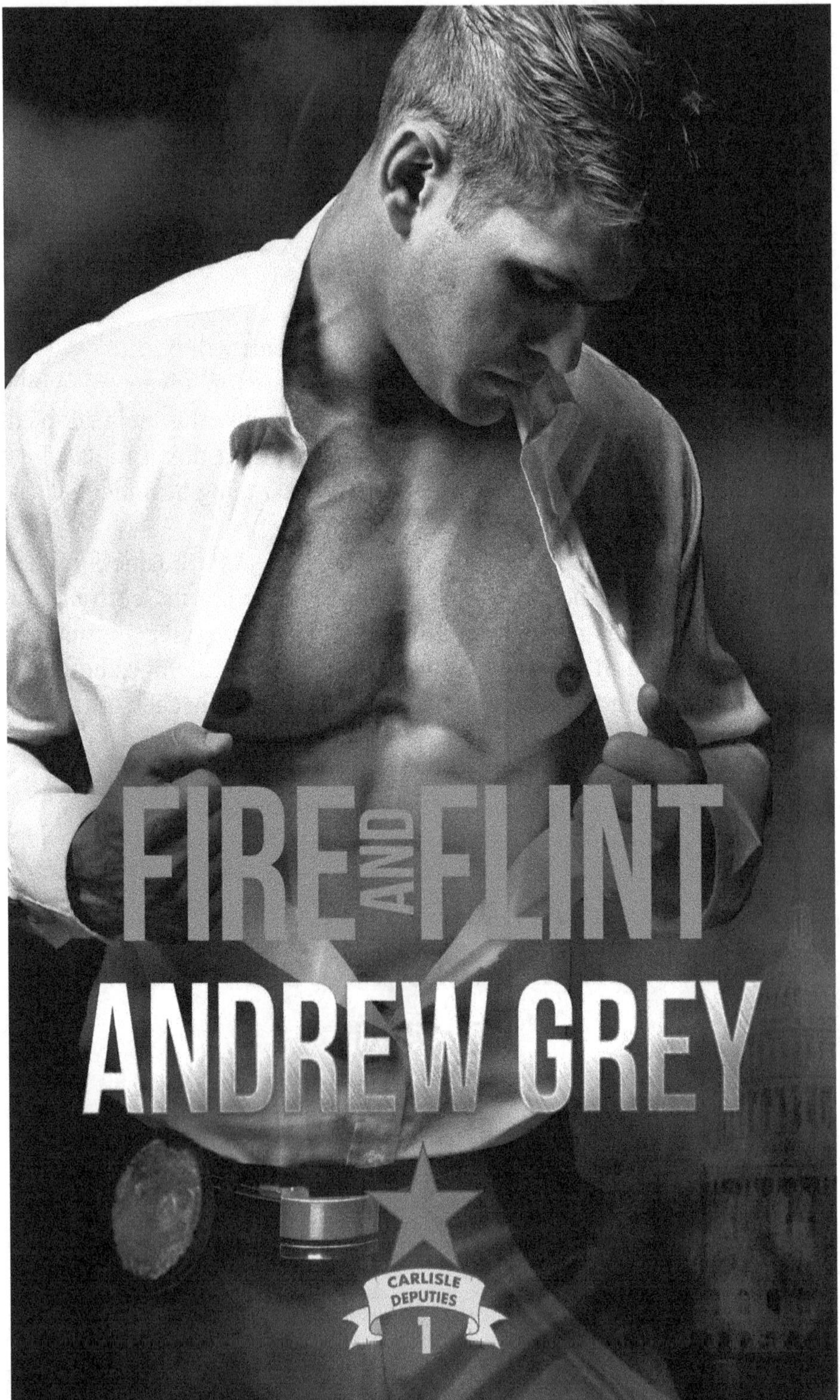
FIRE AND FLINT
ANDREW GREY
CARLISLE DEPUTIES
1

A Carlisle Deputies Novel

Jordan Erichsohn suspects something is rotten about his boss, Judge Crawford. Unfortunately he has nowhere to turn and doubts anyone will believe his claims—least of all the handsome deputy, Pierre Ravelle, who has been assigned to protect the judge after he received threatening letters. The judge has a long reach, and if he finds out Jordan's turned on him, he might impede Jordan adopting his son, Jeremiah.

When Jordan can no longer stay silent, he gathers his courage and tells Pierre what he knows. To his surprise and relief, Pierre believes him, and Jordan finds an ally… and maybe more. Pierre vows to do what it takes to protect Jordan and Jeremiah and see justice done. He's willing to fight for the man he's growing to love and the family he's starting to think of as his own. But Crawford is a powerful and dangerous enemy, and he's not above ripping apart everything Jordan and Pierre are trying to build in order to save himself….

Scan the QR Code
Below to Order!

REKINDLED FLAME

ANDREW GREY

Rekindled Flame: Book One

Firefighter Morgan has worked hard to build a home for himself after a nomadic childhood. When Morgan is called to a fire, he finds the family out front, but their tenant still inside. He rescues Richard Smalley, who turns out to be an old friend he hasn't seen in years and the one person he regretted leaving behind.

Richard has had a hard life. He served in the military, where he lost the use of his legs, and has been struggling to make his way since coming home. Now that he no longer has a place to live, Morgan takes him in, but when someone attempts to set fire to Morgan's house, they both become suspicious and wonder what's going on.

Years ago Morgan was gutted when he moved away, leaving Richard behind, so he's happy to pick things up where they left off. But now that Richard seems to be the target of an arsonist, he may not be the safest person to be around.

SCAN THE QR CODE
BELOW TO ORDER!